Witching Murder

by the same author

Witching Murder

Jennie Melville

St. Martin's Press
New York

Library of Congress Cataloging-in-Publication Data

Melville, Jennie.
    Witching murder / Jennie Melville.
        p.   cm.
    "A Thomas Dunne Book."
    ISBN 0-312-05999-X
    I. Title.
    PR6063.E44W55   1991
    823'.914—dc20   90-27886
                                                                        CIP

First published in Great Britain by Macmillan London Limited.

First U.S. Edition: August 1991
10 9 8 7 6 5 4 3 2 1

Charmian opened a thick white envelope to draw out a card embossed in gold.

WINDSOR CASTLE

I am commanded by Her Majesty to

Charmian put down the card. Naturally, she would accept, that went without saying. One did not turn down Majesty. But she was pleased.

So that's my reward, she thought. I have been a good Royal servant; I detected a canine killer.

But more importantly, I found the murderer of a woman, cleared up the matter of the witches, and no one burnt at the stake.

Never mind a death or two. Or three, if you counted the child.

Chapter One

When you have a cat resident in the house, sooner or later you get to know other people with cats. It is a universal truth. The royal town in Berkshire on the River Thames is particularly heavily provided with cats. Dogs are, of course, the royally established pets, but cats have crept in. There are black cats, pure white cats, black and white cats, striped cats, blotched tabby cats, ginger cats, and cats who are a mixture of all those colours. And these are only the mongrels. There are also the highborn, whose dates of birth and even conceptions are documented: Persian cats, Siamese cats, Burmese cats, Manx cats, Russian Blue cats and British Blue. Also, a new arrival, a large Maine Coon cat who thought, wrongly, that everyone loved him.

Charmian Daniels, policewoman, owned, or was owned by, a pleasant female tabby cat called Muff. Round the corner from where she lived in Maid of Honour Row in Windsor, a neighbour called Winifred Eagle was the possessor of, or was possessed by, a sleek black cat called Benedict. Benedict is a holy and sainted name, but this Benedict was not holy and far from saintly. He held dominion over Abigail Place where Miss Eagle lived. There were only six houses in the little street, each backing on to Maid of Honour Row, each provided with a cat; but all these cats had learnt to know their place.

Sometimes Benedict came across dead things in Miss Eagle's garden, but he always turned aside from them, he was only interested in hunting live creatures. Benedict and Miss Eagle had lived for ten years in the house in Abigail Place before Charmian Daniels moved into Maid of Honour Row; they were old inhabitants.

7

'She's a policewoman, Benny, a Superintendent, I hear,' Winifred had whispered to her black companion, as she groomed him. 'Interesting, isn't it?'

Charmian had bought the house when a move from Deerham Hills together with rapid promotion gave her an important position with the Metropolitan Police in Central London, but no home. To live in Windsor, so close to London yet on the River, which she loved, and in a town so full of character, had taken her fancy. Also, she had friends who lived here, friends both in the town and in the castle precincts. She enjoyed the sociabilities of the small but happy circle in which she moved.

She'd had a long walk from the earnest girl who had taken a good degree at a Scottish university, then joined a county police force with something of a social mission. Even in those early days, when she had worked in the town of Deerham Hills, she had never been content to simply be a police officer; she had always had ambitions. Work as a CID officer had stretched her, she had enjoyed it, known considerable success and promotion. Marriage to a man much senior to her had not dampened her ambition, and indeed her husband had encouraged her until he had been killed.

Had it been a happy marriage? At the time she had thought so, but in retrospect she had wondered – perhaps she had been too ambitious to be a total success as a wife. Slightly gauche, desperately anxious to improve the world and herself with it, that was how she had been. Not easy.

Bits of that old person were still embedded inside her, but success had overlaid them with sophistication. She could afford a good hairdresser now to cut her hair, which had been deep red in early youth and which still had hints of copper; she knew what sort of make-up to use, the kind of understated clothes that suited her.

She managed a reasonable social life; she had especially decided to live in Windsor because an old college friend, Annie Cooper, had settled there, and because she had met a man, distinguished, successful, whom she had thought she

8

could love. She still had a few reservations about Humphrey, but they were melting away.

Winifred had not got her status quite accurate; Charmian was now a Chief Superintendent, and young to be it, although she played down her rank. She specialised in the crimes of women and also crimes against women. There is no such thing as 'women criminals' as a genus, Charmian accepted that view, there are simply women who happen to commit crimes, just as there are men who commit crimes. Nevertheless, there are certain crimes, such as infanticide, that more often women commit and certain crimes, such as rape, that happen more frequently to women. And sometimes, unfashionable as the thought was, Charmian did feel that there were types of woman who became criminals, and interesting types of crime they fell into. In her experience, some of the more complicated and hard to solve murders fell into such a category. Women were so inventive.

The two cats got to know each other first, although apart from scratched noses and torn-out tufts of hair they did not confess to their meetings. But a badly chewed ear is another matter.

The rivals had been quarrelling over a little bundle of bloody something (they could not name what it was).

'Muff!' said Charmian in dismay as she bathed the wounded tabby ear. 'How did you come by this? No, don't answer.' Muff was not about to. 'I know who did it to you, it's that bloody black cat.'

Winifred denied it, of course, and Benedict, like Muff, was saying nothing. He was not built to admit much. If he was capable of saying anything then, 'People do go on,' he would have said.

Charmian, a skilled reader of body language – it was her job, after all, and sometimes her very safety depended upon it – discerned it in his amber eyes.

The little bloodied thing that the animals had been fighting over was tidied up by Miss Eagle. She did not know what it was either, but she had troubled thoughts.

Because she knew it for a hate object.

After that episode, Charmian kept an eye on the household and garden of Winifred, whose corner house was visible from Charmian's back windows. She soon realised that there was a kind of cat track through her hedge into Winifred's that was clearly used by many felines. It had a well-worn look, as if trodden by several generations of paws.

It was possible that other animals used it too: Charmian had seen a fox looking at her over her rubbish bin one early morning. Not a cat-eating fox, she trusted, but it hadn't appeared hungry, quite satisfied with its urban pickings.

Winifred Eagle, her name on the electoral roll where Charmian looked it up, lived alone in her house, but was apparently a sociable soul. Charmian observed three women visitors who came regularly as a group. Perhaps they played bridge together, or possibly it was a small Yoga class. They did not look as if they met to do embroidery together; there was a cheerful, healthy, unfashionable air to them. Perhaps a touch of eccentricity in their clothes. Sometimes they erupted from the house with bursts of loud laughter which could be heard round the corner; sometimes they came out quietly, arm in arm. She felt they had a rich and vigorous life of their own.

The three regulars were a woman with curly red hair, one with a crop going nicely grey, and a plump attractive girl with long blonde hair, who was much the youngest and of whom the others seemed protective. A more varied cast of women came and went, but it was clear that whatever drew the group together, these four were the core.

A well-built man, younger than the women who were all, except for the fair girl, of early middle age, occasionally seemed to join the party.

Charmian noticed once or twice another visitor, whose face she recognised as that of a young local policewoman. This interested her.

She would see this girl at the approaching twice-yearly meeting of the Professional Women's Inter-Discipline Discussion Club, where doctors, lawyers, policewomen and social workers met to pool their knowledge and talk over their problems. Dolly, now a detective sergeant, usually attended.

Charmian had time for speculation at the moment, she was enduring – enjoyment did not come into it – a short spell of leave.

She moved her right hand experimentally. It seemed supple and agile enough but it had found out how to evade her orders. She looked at her pen but decided not to try it. Leave it, she could always dictate a letter, or pick it out on the word processor.

A married woman crouched over the body of the woman, whom she called X or left nameless, in the kitchen of X's house. She was happy to think of the victim as X. X marked the spot. She stretched X out, the blood from the stab wound had almost ceased to flow, but still oozed somewhat. She arranged the limbs neatly, not bothering to hide the knife, which was indeed from X's own kitchen. She had tied the wrists loosely together. This was her own touch. How she felt about the victim. It signified submission. Victory for one woman, defeat for the other. And that was definitely how she felt.

The woman arranged various cult objects about the body. A bunch of twigs, a little leather bag containing unseen trifles, a bundle of brown hair, and at the head a small, furry, dead body. Four black candles, two at the head of the body, two at the feet. Unlit. Then she left.

Later that day a married man let himself into the house to which he had a key. He stood staring at what he saw. He felt sick at the sight, a great wave of nausea swept over him and he swayed where he stood. He went to the sink and vomited.

He left X where she lay, but removed several of the objects, dropping them in the sink, and released her hands. He left the rat, which he could not bring himself to touch.

'Someone else will have to report you dead, my dear,' he said under his breath. Then he left the house and went to his car, which he had parked round the corner as he always did. Tears were rolling down his face as he drove away. He had never felt more fearful. How terrible women were both in love and in revenge.

On the same day, but in the late afternoon, Denise Flaxon, a beauty consultant, rang the bell. She worked for Elysium Creams as a saleswoman, visiting clients in their own homes.

She had promised to come at this time on this day, bringing with her a range of cosmetics and face treatment creams for the woman inside. She had promised Miss Vivien Charles that she would have a chance to model the cosmetics as the firm she represented was looking for a new face for a new campaign. This was not strictly true but it got Denise in and helped sales.

No one answered the bell, so she gave the door a tentative push. It opened before her and she went in.

The door to the kitchen was wide open. Her eyes went wide, she gave a genuine and spontaneous scream of surprise at what she saw.

She knew at once there was something terribly terribly wrong here. She too felt sick, she could smell the vomit in the sink, saw the objects that had been dumped there, but she controlled herself.

She did not touch the rat. There must have been a grave and rabid infection inside that rat for it to have gone so swollen and rotten so soon.

She knew what she had to do, and reluctantly she set about doing it. She was tempted to run away, never to be seen in the neighbourhood again, but the death was a public fact that had to be acknowledged.

She could not bring herself to touch the telephone in this house, so she went to the call box in the street outside to dial the police. She had noticed it on an earlier visit.

'Dulcet Road, number six. Merrywick. You know where that is?'

They told her to wait there, so she stood in the sun by her own car, a small Ford Fiesta, waiting. She knew how to wait.

12

'Don't touch anything,' they said.

'Wouldn't think of it,' she told herself.

She was still there, patient and still, when the police car arrived.

These first officers were two uniformed patrolmen. Denise refused to enter the house with them.

'No, I'm not going in there again. You can talk to me out here or in your car.'

The two men went into the house together. Soon, one of them emerged to make a telephone call from the car. Denise watched in silence.

'The CID is coming over, it's their pigeon. Murder all right, isn't it?' He was a young man, talking more than he should have done, a measure of his shock at what he had seen.

'I think so,' said Denise.

'You can make your statement to the Sergeant.'

'I'd like to go home.'

'After that,' he said with sympathy. 'We'll give you a lift, if necessary. Nasty for you. Not what you'd be expecting.'

'No,' said Denise tersely.

'Come and sit in the car.'

But Denise preferred the fresh air. 'I'll sit here.' And she sank on to the brick wall of the garden. She was not unaware that by this time several neighbours were taking a discreet interest in what was going on. She kept her eyes firmly turned away from them.

From her perch on the wall she observed a man with a bag arrive, whom she took to be the police surgeon, and then a young woman drove up and went into the house.

Dulcet Road, North Haw, Merrywick, was a new development, nearer Slough than Eton or Windsor, with a pleasant country air to it. Number six was a small but pretty house, one of a group designed by the architect to be a single-person dwelling, but prices had risen so fast in Merrywick lately that several young families were crammed into them.

Detective Sergeant (CID) Dolly Barstow marched into

13

the kitchen to take charge. She brought with her a young detective constable whom she was training in her ways.

'Now then, what have you got to show me?'

Then she took a look. 'Ah,' she said thoughtfully. It was a shock to her. Be a shock to anyone, what we've got here, she told herself. Nevertheless, for her there was an added element of surprise.

She walked over to the body to stand staring down. She studied the tricks that had been laid out round the body. The candles were still there, the little bag of nameless objects, and the rat. The rest were in the sink, but she had not seen them yet. 'How very nasty.'

The police surgeon provided the unnecessary information that the victim had been stabbed, that it had not been suicide, and that the time of death was to be guessed at as about six or eight hours earlier. The pathologist would no doubt offer a more precise opinion after autopsy.

Dolly looked at the clock. It was now four o'clock, so the woman had been killed that morning.

'Round about breakfast time, then. Live alone, did she?'

No one answered, no one had any idea. But Dolly believed it was so.

'She's wearing outdoor clothes. She must have been planning to go out.' Dolly raised her head. 'I suppose she did live here?'

The uniformed officer from the car found his voice. 'The lady who found her says she was calling by appointment.'

'Selling something, was she?' Dolly had noticed the figure with its pretty pink briefcase propped up against the wall.

'Face creams, Sergeant.'

'Oh.' Dolly was interested, she was having skin troubles herself. Suddenly she seemed allergic to her usual foundation lotion. She put up her hand to touch one of the rough patches on her cheeks. 'I'll get her statement.' Before the Inspector comes, she thought. She was not too keen on Fred Elman, with whom she was teamed; their styles did not match.

Dolly went outside where Denise Flaxon was still seated

14

on the wall, looking as if someone had hit her on the head.

'Sorry to keep you waiting, you've had a bad shock I can see, Miss . . .' Dolly hesitated.

'Mrs Flaxon,' said Denise automatically, as if she were programmed to give the right answers. 'I'm a widow.'

'Mrs Flaxon, I'm afraid I have to ask questions and get a statement. Will you come inside the house?'

'No.' Denise shook her head. 'Not going in there.'

'The car, then?'

Denise assented to the police car. The two women sat in the back, with the sunlight falling on Mrs Flaxon's face so that she kept putting up her hand as if to brush the light rays aside.

'Would you like to move out of the sun, Mrs Flaxon?' Dolly wanted to put the woman at her ease if she could. Elman, when he came later, would be no rest cure. Charm and ease of manner did not make up the Inspector's style.

'No, I'm all right here. Let's get on with it.' In the strong light the woman looked older than she had done at first glance, with lines around the eyes and mouth. She had a clear pale skin, carefully made up. Dark brown hair with pale brown eyes that looked almost grey as she moved her head to put on dark spectacles. Nose just a little too thick for sheer beauty, and the cheeks too fat, but personable.

Dolly got her name and address down quickly.

She was Mrs Denise Flaxon; she lived at Woodstock Close, Slough.

'Business address?'

'I work from there. I have an area franchise with Elysium Creams, also Perlita Perfumes.' Just for a moment she gave a quick professional look at Dolly's face and Dolly felt the impact. 'I cover Merrywick. I visited her.' She did not commit herself to a name as if it might be dangerous. 'I visited the house by appointment.' She stopped.

'Go on.'

'No one answered the door. I knew I was expected, so after waiting a bit I tried the door. It wasn't locked so I went in.' She stopped again.

'So you went in? Into the kitchen?'

'Not straight away. I stood in the hall, I think I called out. Then I went into the kitchen . . . She was lying on the floor. Lots of blood, the knife beside her. I didn't touch it . . . Nor those other things.' She looked at Dolly. 'You saw them?'

Dolly nodded.

'The . . . That's witchcraft,' she whispered. 'Black magic.'

I doubt it, thought Dolly. Looks like plain old murder to me with nasty undertones, but she had several things to think about on these lines herself. She knew a witch or two, and possibly now it was a pity she did.

'And then?' she prompted.

'I nearly ran away,' said Denise, speaking no more than the honest truth. But someone had seen her go into the house. 'But in the end, I went and called the police from the call box at the end of the road.' She nodded towards it.

'Were you sick?'

'No. Felt it, but I wasn't.'

Someone had been, though; sick in the kitchen sink. The murderer?

'Thank you, Mrs Flaxon. We'll have to get all this written down and you'll have to sign it. I'll send you down to the station and you can make your statement there.'

'Will you come with me?'

'I can't do that, but I promise you we will be as quick as we can. Then you can go home. We may get in touch with you at home later.'

Mrs Flaxon departed to make her statement, and in due course was allowed to leave the Merrywick Police Station. She drove herself home to Slough, skirting the crowded roads, taking a back route, driving past the street in which a shop called Twickers was still open. Woodstock Close, where she lived, was just around the corner.

Dolly went back into the house to seize the services of DC Madden. She was interrupted by the arrival of Inspector Elman. He was new to the area, having been transferred on promotion from a country district. But he was a born Londoner who just happened to have found

16

his career in a force outside the Met. He was streetwise, careful of himself and occasionally distrustful. Well, always distrustful, especially of his colleagues who were women.

'I've just come in to see what's what, but I won't be staying. I've still got my hands full with the Durham Flats business.' This was a multiple killing among a group of Asian families in Slough. 'You are going to head the team on this, Barstow.'

Dolly was half pleased, half annoyed. She knew she was up for promotion, but she hated to be beholden to Fred Elman for anything. If he didn't trust her, she didn't trust him. Mutual.

'I'll be in nominal charge, of course.'

Of course. And Superintendent Father would be over him. But the Superintendent had responsibility for a big arson case just coming into court and would not be seen much.

Any credit, however, for a successful conclusion to the case would go to those two, and any failure, to her. But Dolly knew the rules, and also how to bend them to her own advantage, if she had to.

'Right,' she said.

'All reports to me, of course. Looks like a simple domestic killing from what I hear.'

He had not seen the objects arranged around the body, of course, Dolly reflected.

'Get it tidied up fast and we'll all be home and dry.'

Dolly nodded.

'Well, look pleased, girl. Could do you good.'

Dolly considered how to put what she had to say.

'There's one complication. I knew her. We were not friends, but we've met.'

Two evenings later, the two women, Dolly and Charmian, met at the Discussion Club in Windsor; both of them glad to see the other, on the look-out for each other without admitting it.

The discussion group always met in the beautiful upstairs

17

room of the Cumberland Hall in Sheet Street, Windsor, where the panelling and the portraits of ancient dignitaries gave you something to look at if the debate palled.

Sherry glass in hand, Dolly approached Charmian as she stood beneath a portrait of Lord North, Prime Minister to George III and one of the chief reasons for the loss of the North American colonies, and whose portrait by James Treharne is appropriately wooden.

'The sherry seems better this month,' said Dolly.

'I saw to it myself.' Charmian had developed a taste for dry sherry, one not shared by all the group, many of whom, in spite of their worldly success and polished, sophisticated appearances, still retained a liking for sweeter and even fizzy drinks. 'I laid in some cream sherry for those who prefer it, though.'

'What is the subject under discussion tonight?'

'Women and equal opportunities in the professions. I can see blood being drawn. I shall probably add some myself.'

Dolly sipped her sherry; she really liked gin herself, but had learnt to drink what she was offered, something she felt sure that Charmian had never done. 'Can I talk to you afterwards? I need advice.'

'Sure. I want to talk to you too.'

'Oh?' Dolly was thoughtful as she took her seat under a portrait of the young William Lamb, Lord Melbourne.

Afterwards, over plates of curried chicken, Dolly said, 'You first.'

Charmian took a drink of water, the curry was exceptionally hot. 'I'm interested in the woman who lives in the corner house in Abigail Place.' She saw a flash of recognition in Dolly's face. 'Interested in her friends too. What goes on there, Dolly? I've seen you there.'

'Have you? Thought you might have done. Thought I saw you looking once.' Dolly put down the food which was suddenly unappealing to her. 'I'm interested in what goes on there too, as a matter of fact. I keep my eye on things; I'd heard talk and I wanted to know what it amounted to.'

Dolly grinned. 'Preventive police work, you could call it. Also, I was curious.'

'What sort of talk?'

'About what the women got up to. The inhabitants of the Great Park complained they were worshipping a tree and performing rites round it. That's how I got to know.'

'And were they?'

'Not exactly. But they'd had a sort of service round the oak on Midsummer's Eve. And then Caprice Dash has a shop in Slough where she sells a mixture of organic fruit and veg, herbal stuff and vitamin supplements, and some funny odds and ends as well. I thought there might be drugs in it somewhere.' She added thoughtfully, 'But I'm bound to say I haven't caught a whiff of anything like that. They seem a healthy bunch.'

'And who are they?'

'The four women. Winifred Eagle, you know her.' Charmian nodded. 'Then there's Alice Peacock, and Caprice Dash. And a small group of other women who come and go. And then there's Vivien Charles. She's younger than the others.'

'I had noticed. And there's a man at times.'

'Yes, Mr Fox.'

'So what does go on?'

Dolly took a swig of sherry, considered a mouthful of curry, and then said, 'They call themselves witches. They're a coven.'

Charmian was silent. Then she said, 'A small one.'

'Size doesn't matter.'

'And what about you?'

'I said I was just interested. They said I could watch. I was a kind of initiate. Like Vivien. I don't think she was that keen really.' Lonely, she had thought of Vivien; lonely and not secure.

'Do they know you are a police officer?'

'No, but I think Mrs Dash suspects. I don't know if they'd mind. They are strangely open in a funny kind of way.' She sounded as if she liked the women. 'And, of course, they

19

could have been laughing at me all the time. Having a joke at my expense. Sometimes I have thought they were.'

'And the man?'

'Well, just as nuns have to have a priest, he was their kind of priest. Apparently you have to have one. Or sometimes.'

'So what did they do?'

'It seemed quite harmless,' said Dolly slowly. 'White magic, earth stuff. Quite nice really. Nothing dangerous. Or so I thought.'

'Yes,' Charmian studied Dolly's face. 'Well, you've told me what I wanted to know. And why you were there.' It was the sort of thing a keen young policewoman might do, but with its embarrassing side as a confession. Dolly obviously found it so. 'What did you want to ask me?'

'I was called to the scene of a murder a couple of days ago. A woman had been stabbed in her own kitchen. I knew her as soon as I looked at her. It was Viv.'

The young woman with the long blonde hair and the Renoir face was dead. She had been a beauty, with something innocent about her, thought Charmian – a country girl, a village beauty. And then, more cynically, but I only saw her across the garden fence, she could have been anything.

And she had been murdered. Victims are sometimes made, self-made at that, not chosen at random. There has to be a reason.

'It was a shock,' Dolly said. 'I liked the girl. And there she was, laid out on her own kitchen floor with some nasty-looking objects laid out all round her.'

Soberly, Dolly said, 'It looked wicked.'

'What is it you want from me?' asked Charmian.

'Advice. A chance to talk it over with you. It's going to be my case.'

Thoughtfully, Charmian said, 'I'd like to see the house. I'd like to go to Merrywick and have a look.'

Chapter Two

The two women drove out through Windsor and took the road which circled Eton and led to Merrywick.

Merrywick called itself a village. It had a post office, a library, a school, a church and a butcher's shop, all of which made it a real village and a fortunate one. However, only the church and one house was old, truly old, the rest had been built in the last ten years to house a large population of prosperous people who liked to live there because it was near Windsor and Eton (not to mention two good girls' schools), but whose professional lives were spent in London. To the purist, Merrywick was thus not a true village but a gimcrack modern imitation. Naturally the Merrywickers resented this bitterly and being a highly educated and articulate lot found ways of expressing this.

Dulcet Road, where Vivien Charles had been found in pools of blood in her own kitchen, was a cul-de-sac of small houses, built in imitation Regency style with little iron balconies at the first-floor window and a minute curving flight of steps to the front door. They were tiny, spurious, pretend, but they had a kind of doll's house charm. Every front door was a different colour, and Vivien's was yellow.

There were heavy footprints all over the front garden but no sign of the police presence otherwise. However, Charmian noticed at least one front-window curtain twitch as they drove up. The neighbours were on the watch, and who could blame them?

Charmian stopped the car and sat there looking at the prospect before her. 'Before we go in, let's talk a bit. How did you get to know these women? In fact, start at the beginning, what put you on to them in the first place?'

'Oh, gossip, hearsay, you know how things go round,' said Dolly lightly. 'A Yoga class starting here, a new dance and exercise club opening there, people talk about it, that sort of thing. This came into that category. I think I heard at the hairdressers. The girl who did my hair said she had a neighbour who claimed to be a witch. She didn't seem to mind, she thought it was funny. I thought it might not be.'

'Go on.'

'Then when I was in Merrywick Library I saw a woman taking out a book called *The Affair of the Poisons*. The librarian said it was about witchcraft in the reign of Louis XIV of France. I thought the borrower might be the witch. So I followed her. She went to a shop in Slough called Twickers.'

'Funny name for a shop.'

'Funny shop. But I think the name means something. It was selling books on the occult, books on witchcraft, and all sorts of odds and ends to do with it. Herbs, spices, crystal balls, black candles, specially prepared mirrors, the lot. The woman in charge told me very firmly that she only dealt in white witchcraft . . . the old religion, she called it. And I'm bound to say it looked quite harmless, a kind of cross between a health food shop of a rustic sort and a toy shop.'

'What happened to the woman you followed?'

'She bought a box of candles and went off. It didn't matter because I was talking to Caprice Dash who turned out to own the shop and she invited me to their next meeting.'

'Of their coven?'

'She didn't call it that. But I suppose it was.'

'Trusting of her to invite you just like that.'

'I must have a nice face,' said Dolly. She got out of the car. 'Anyway, that's how I met them.'

'Sounds too easy,' said Charmian thoughtfully. She followed Dolly out of the car and they stood at the gate looking up the narrow garden path. It wasn't a garden anyone had put any love into, so it had a sad neglected air with a few dejected roses and some unwatered window boxes. A bed of geraniums was doing well, but Charmian knew that geraniums thrived on neglect.

'In a way it was. I found out later that Winifred Eagle, whose house they mostly used, had seen in her Tarot Cards that a girl like me was coming into their lives. Make what you like of that,' said Dolly, who hadn't quite enjoyed being the answer to the witch's vision. It made her skin itch. Her face was sore now, and she moved her head uneasily. 'I went to the first meeting and met the others – Alice Peacock and Vivien, and a couple of other women who seemed to have just dropped in. We didn't do anything much, just talk and prayers to what they called The Female One. We prayed for me, for my good fortune, which embarrassed me; I'm still wondering if the prayers were answered.' Because there was no doubt that if this case went well, her career would prosper.

But on account of the death of one of the little group? It just confirmed Dolly's belief that you should be careful what you prayed for.

'Did you pray?' asked Charmian, curious to find out exactly what all this had meant to her young friend.

'No, I'm a Methodist,' said Dolly prosaically. 'I just kept my mouth shut. But the She they were praying to sounded a decent sort. For women, if you see what I mean. They said it was the 'old religion'. That made it white magic, the good stuff. The black magic outfit try to have a word with the Devil. Take your pick.'

'There must be something about these women: I've been interested in them, you've been interested in them, and now they've had a murder,' said Charmian as they walked up the path to the house. 'Have you got a key to the house?'

'Of course.' Dolly produced one.

Charmian studied the scene. It looked quiet enough, too quiet really, for she saw no sign of a protective police presence. Dolly observed this and spoke up:

'All the forensics have been done, so the team's cleared

23

out. We are a bit overstretched at the moment, but a patrol car comes round regularly.'

'Where do the other women live?'

'Well, Winifred Eagle, you know about, she's your neighbour, and the other two, Caprice Dash and Alice Peacock, they call her Birdie, both live in Merrywick. Dash in a block of flats overlooking the River and Peacock in a bungalow in Garter Road. The bungalow is called The Nest,' said Dolly with a straight face.

'A bunch of characters.'

'Apart from being, well, what they claimed to be, they seemed quite ordinary, comfortable women. They could have been members of the Women's Institute and the Conservative Party. In fact, for all I know, they are. Birdie certainly makes good scones and jam. I had some once, and I'd bet that she votes for Mrs Thatcher. In fact, I've had the sort of feeling once or twice that she mixes her up with The Great Mother.' She was fumbling with the door lock. 'The key's sticking.'

'Something wrong with the lock?'

'It's a new lock. I had all the locks replaced, just in case.'

While Dolly was struggling with the door, Charmian walked round the flight of steps to look in at a window.

She found she was surveying a long, narrow sitting room with a view to the garden beyond, visible through a pretty set of glass doors which managed to look both Victorian, phoney and charming at the same time. Real skill had gone into creating this pretend scene, she thought.

The room, clear to her view, was plainly furnished as if the occupant had not long moved in and was undecided about what would make her comfortable. The floor was covered in plain, pale carpeting, on which rested several upright chairs and a severe-looking sofa. A portable television set stood on a painted round table. As far as Charmian could see there were no curtains on either of the windows, front or back.

It was evening, dark, but with a bright moon. She could see enough.

'Probably as well there are no curtains,' she found herself thinking. 'If one of them moved, in the moonlight, in the house where there had been a murder, even I might feel a shiver.'

The thought was so unlike her that she drew it back rapidly and popped it into a deep drawer inside her mind.

Then she thought, 'But I can see into this room too well.'

A soft red light suffused the room.

'Got the door open,' called Dolly.

'Come over here, will you, I can see a light. Red light.'

Dolly hurried over. 'Not a fire, is it?' she asked in alarm.

'No.'

No, the light was too steady and quiet, not a flicker in it.

'Coming from the kitchen,' said Dolly. 'Well, let's get in there and look.'

She pushed open the front door, hesitated for a moment, then went in. Charmian stayed looking.

'The light's gone.'

And it had, there was no light at all now, except that coming from the street lamp.

She followed Dolly into the house, which smelt at once cold and stuffy.

Dolly put up a hand to the wall switch and flooded the hall with a clear white glare from a central lamp. 'Perhaps it was some sort of optical illusion.'

'Rubbish. I saw it,' said Charmian. 'And so did you. Turn out the light so we can look.'

'There it is again.'

Now they could both see a soft red glow from the kitchen. Charmian went forward.

On one wall of the kitchen there was a plug which glowed.

'Damn,' said Dolly with relief. 'I know what that is. It's a kind of safety plug. Used in nurseries, that sort of thing. You can burn it night and day. In the daytime I suppose I didn't notice it. Wonder why she had it?'

'Didn't like the dark?'

'Not sure if I like it myself,' said Dolly. 'Not in this place.'

'Says something about both of us, the way we reacted,'

said Charmian. Or perhaps it was the house. Certainly there was something disagreeable about its ordinariness. She would not want to live there herself.

She put the kitchen light on. A long narrow strip of tubing over a central cooking area opened the room up with a cold dazzle. There was a window with a view of the garden over the sink, while on the right-hand wall there was a door with glass panels which led to an outer lobby.

'She had a deep freeze out there,' said Dolly. 'And there's a door to the garden.'

'Anything in the deep freeze?'

'Empty.'

On the floor was the chalked shape where Vivien had sprawled.

'She was on her back with her arms on her body?'

Dolly nodded. 'Yes. Head slightly to one side. To the left, as you see. It wasn't a natural pose. She'd been laid out.' Dolly paused. 'It's part of what I didn't like.' Only part of it though, she decided. 'And then there were these objects laid out round her. Some of them had been moved and put in the sink, but you could see where they'd been.'

'Witchcraft symbols?'

Dolly hesitated. 'Could have been. I don't know enough about it to be sure.'

'Are you all right, Dolly? I don't mean here and now, but in yourself, in general.'

'Yes, why?'

'Just the way you look.'

'Well, a bit loveless,' Dolly admitted. She leaned against the sink. 'You know how it goes.'

Charmian nodded. She did know.

'I suppose I was interested in these women and their white magic. Wanted to see what it amounted to. If it worked.'

'And did it?'

'I don't know. I half thought it did.'

'But you're a professional!' Charmian was incredulous. 'You don't think like that. Nature doesn't deal in magic.'

'Call it a professional interest,' said Dolly drily. 'Shall we go?'

She seemed to want to get away. Which is exactly what worries me, Charmian told herself.

'Not finished yet,' she said.

Charmian walked round the kitchen, studying it. Apart from signs of police activity it was neat enough, with the same unused, uncared for look of the rest of the house. Whatever else about her, she was willing to guess that Vivien had not been a happy woman.

On the kitchen table was a cardboard box.

'What's this?'

Dolly took off the lid. 'This must have got left behind. Damn.' Inside the box was a small, black sodden object. Vaguely humanoid in shape, with a shock of hair. It seemed to be made of black wax, probably a candle, melted, then shaped into a little creature.

'We had to get the plumber in.'

'Oh, why?'

'The lavatory was blocked. When the chap put his arm down he pulled that doll out. She must have tried to flush it away.'

'Don't wonder, gave her a shock, I should think. This looks like black magic,' said Charmian, picking up the malevolent little object.

Then she said, 'I'm going upstairs for a look round.'

'You won't find much. Only one room is furnished. The Forensics discovered no blood traces. Not much of anything. It's a bedroom. Viv slept there, of course, so there are her clothes and make-up. Then there's the bathroom. Bit spartan and very clean.'

'You stay here. I'll go up.'

Dolly nodded. 'Right.'

Her manner troubled Charmian. 'Is there something you're not telling me?'

'Not about the women,' said Dolly slowly, as if she could say more, wanted too, indeed, but needed encouragement.

'The man, then? The one they call their warlock?'

27

'If he is one,' said Dolly. 'I don't know what to make of him. But he has something. And I think I've fallen for him.'

'Does he know? I mean, have you . . . ' Charmian hesitated.

'Oh no, nothing like that. I haven't and he hasn't. But he may know. He's quick enough. And it's clouding my judgement. That's why I wanted your help.'

It had taken long enough for her to get it out. But no easy confession to make.

'I'd like to meet him,' said Charmian. 'All of them, in fact. I shall need to if I am going to help. And it ought to be cleared officially. I'm on leave at the moment.' As you probably know, but she did not say so aloud.

Dolly hesitated. She knew something of what had happened to Charmian, it had been talked about.

Two months earlier the boyfriend of a woman whom Charmian had put away for armed robbery had tried first to rape and then shoot her. In the struggle, Charmian had shot him dead. The inquiry that followed cleared her completely, she was praised for her bravery, her work did not suffer, she felt unmoved. Then one day when she picked up her pen, her hand simply refused to write.

Working police officers do not have this sort of illness, so she carried on, tapping out her work notes on the typewriter with her left hand. For all other uses, such as eating, the other hand seemed willing.

A thorough medical examination revealed nothing wrong physically. 'Your body is telling you something, I'm not sure what,' said the examining doctor. 'But the best thing I can advise is to take a holiday.' A psychologist, trained to deal with the traumas of police officers after a killing, was at hand to help, but he saw at once that this woman would resist the suggestion, she needed careful handling.

Charmian had leave due to her. She took a month. Within the first week she was bored stiff.

It was probably written all over her and Dolly could see it. 'I'll work on it,' Dolly said. 'I have approached Elman already, not my best friend but he has his good side. You are the expert on women and crime. And the Force has used you before.'

'It's what I'm here for,' said Charmian.

She stood there thinking. Something that had been resting below the surface of her consciousness suddenly rose up. 'But why did the light seem to go out?'

'I've been wondering that,' admitted Dolly.

Charmian said slowly, 'Someone could have been standing in front of it.'

'What?'

'And then moved away.' She put up a hand. 'Can you feel a draught?'

She moved over to open the inner door of the kitchen. The back door was swinging slightly in a night breeze.

'Someone has been here.'

And had now gone.

Charmian examined the lock: it had not been forced. 'Thought you said you had the locks changed?'

'I did.'

'Who else has got keys, then?'

'I gave a set to an estate agents. Blood and Sons. Vivien only rented this place. They said they needed them.'

'I think you may have made a mistake there,' said Charmian, straightening herself. 'All the same, I don't think it was someone from the estate agents who was round here tonight. You'll have to check.' She began to move round the kitchen. 'Anything changed here? Anything gone?'

'No, all looks the same.'

'What about the sitting room?'

Dolly went to make a survey, presently returning to shake her head. 'I can't see that anything's been touched.'

Miserably she felt her career was taking a rapid dive down to nowhere.

'We'd better look upstairs.'

The bathroom door was wide open, but was empty of everything except soap and towels. A set of blue towels and a set in white. Both looked dry and untouched.

In the bedroom, however, several drawers in the dressing table had been pulled open.

By the bed, the frilled pink lamp had been knocked over and with the impact the light had come on.

'He or she was up here,' said Charmian.

Dolly was morose. 'We missed something. Or he wouldn't have had to come back to collect it.' She gave a despondent shrug. 'I'm not going to enjoy writing the report on this.'

She was first down the stairs. 'Nothing like this has ever happened to me before.'

It felt like a rotten plot to ruin her. This had definitely never happened to her before.

Someone had put a spell on her.

As Dolly went through the back door to check on the garden, Charmian followed.

By the freezer, a small upright chest, she paused. The door was slightly ajar.

'Did you say the freezer was empty?'

'Yes,' Dolly called back.

'Well, it's not now.'

Charmian opened the door wider. Inside, bolt upright, tail lashing, emerald green eyes shining, sat a big black cat.

He sprang past her with a curse, lashing out with his paw at her as he went, drawing blood.

'You devil,' said Charmian.

Chapter Three

'I'll help you in this case,' said Charmian, as they stood outside the house in Dulcet Road. 'Semi-officially, of course, but you'll still have to clear it with the powers that be. No treading on toes.' Or not more than she could help. She would probably do so anyway, it had been a knack of hers all through her working life, but at least she had prepared her defences. This she had learnt to do; Dolly, she thought, was still learning. Women had to learn more and harder, that seemed to be the rule, and no kicking it.

I'm doing this for Dolly Barstow, she told herself, not because I am bored, not because I am madly interested in this troupe of white witches – Eagle, Peacock and the rest – and certainly not because I am terrified of thinking about my slightly dead right hand. Which was actually rather sore and hot this day, as if it was still taking an interest in life, albeit a painful one. This sense of its independent life was a secret she nursed inside her. Not the sort of thing you said aloud, not if you were a working police officer with a reputation for sanity to hang on to.

'I'm grateful,' said Dolly, who in general hated admitting gratitude to anyone. 'Tomorrow I have to be in court, but I'll let you have a copy of what material I have got so far. The scientific stuff is slow coming in as usual, of course.' All the police scientific departments were apt to cry that they were overworked or that their computer was hiccuping and they ought to have another, if not two. All true, no doubt, but fruitful cause for strife. 'Keep it to yourself, of course.'

Charmian nodded. 'Of course. What happened to the cat?'

'Got away,' said Dolly briefly. It would do, cats like that

did, a professional escaper if ever she saw one. Probably far away and in another country by now.

'Where will you start?' she asked, as she dropped Charmian back at her house in Maid of Honour Row. Even as she put the question, she realised she was being tactless. You didn't talk that way to a distinguished colleague like Charmian Daniels. It just showed how this case was getting to her.

But Charmian took no offence. 'With your notes and the work you've done already. Then I'd like to find out how someone entered the house in Dulcet Road. You've got a key. So have the estate agents. I might take a look at them.'

A flat package dropped through Charmian's letterbox early next morning while she and Muff were still asleep. Dolly Barstow had made an early start.

Muff, catlike, heard the noise at the door and trotted down to inspect. Nothing to eat, she decided sadly. Could have been a dead mouse or a bird delivered by a kindly God, one should always be on the look out for such things, although God usually handed such offerings on a special blue plate. She sniffed delicately at the package: a dull smell.

Her duty done, she returned to the bedroom to awake God with a patted paw which felt, if you were on the receiving side of it, like cotton wool with pins in it, thus to remind Charmian that a day begun with a saucer of warm milk was a day begun well.

'Coming.' Charmian heaved herself from the bed; she was putting on weight lately, not much, but noticeable, and it annoyed her. A side-effect of idleness. 'Milk for you, coffee for me.'

On the way to the kitchen she picked up the post, which had now arrived, together with the newspaper, and Dolly Barstow's packet.

There was a card from Humphrey in the post: he had been absent for two months in Washington, occupied on one of those important but nameless missions that engaged him. He knew what had taken place in Charmian's life, about which he had telephoned and sent loving letters, but he had not come home. She accepted it, work was work, but it rankled. Perhaps this was part of her trouble. She wanted, in the most feminine and uncharacteristic way, to come first above everything with him.

The kitchen was a friendly, pleasant room where Charmian spent a lot of her time. Under the influence of her god-child and occasional lodger, Kate Cooper (an architectural student at present in Delhi observing the imperial buildings of Lutyens), Charmian had remodelled it and could now sit here admiring her high tech pipes and drains. She sometimes lost her way among all her equipment, some unused, but on the whole she was proud of herself for having achieved it. Considering its apparent simplicity of design it had been amazingly expensive.

Today she found her way unerringly to the new coffee machine which ground the beans before delivering the brew. She could pour coffee and butter toast with her right hand. How strange that it refused to write her name.

Dolly Barstow's folder of documents told her what she needed to know.

First, the neutral, toneless medical report.

Vivien Charles had died from one major stab wound to the chest, delivered with some force, but she had also received several other savage punctures in her throat and abdomen, from any one of which she might have died, had not the blood spurted so speedily from a main artery.

She had been attacked from the front, the attacker standing close to her. From the angle of the wounds, it could be deduced that the attacker was taller than the victim. The shape of the wounds fitted in with the knife found beside her. This knife appeared to be one of a set of Sabatier kitchen knives hanging on the kitchen wall.

After she had breakfasted while reading Dolly's dossier, Charmian dressed herself in what she called her 'Windsor working clothes', summer-style: a cream linen skirt, a pale shirt and matching sweater. They were the sort of outfit that all the local women wore and made her unnoticeable and anonymous.

Then she strolled round the corner to where Miss Eagle lived. A very ordinary house with a well-kept garden, perhaps running to herbs rather than flowers but otherwise normal. Odd to think that a modern witch lived here.

'Owned or rented from Blood and Son?' she thought. But it looked like a freehold property, totally witch-owned.

Presently she saw Miss Eagle advancing into the garden, armed with a pair of secateurs to do some pruning, although it was not yet the season for pruning.

Miss Eagle, who had picked up the secateurs because she had observed Charmian, snipped away angrily at an innocent hydrangea which would regret it later in the year. 'Snooping. What's she up to?'

Her cat wandered up and the two of them watched Charmian watching them.

Estate agents had proliferated in Windsor and its environs lately, together with building societies to finance what the agents sold. Sometimes they were combined under one roof. Merrywick had three such firms.

Peter and Paul Ellistons, a very bright young firm who had cleverly established themselves next door to Florence's Old Curiosity Shop, in which indeed Peter had money. In fact, he was Florence, more or less, there being no other.

Down the street was London and National, brash and new, not really smart enough for Merrywick but doing very well because their salesmen never gave up. So they claimed.

Blood and Sons were the third firm and had been there the longest. They still retained the air of a genteel, old, established agency, but a small notice in the window revealed that it was now part of a chain called Homeline.

A large, gleaming car was parked on a double yellow line as Charmian drove up, but it had the confident air of a car to whom no one ever gave a parking ticket. Charmian looked round hopefully for a traffic warden to point out the offender, but of course there never was one in Merrywick.

In the front office a young woman, auburn-haired and with big greenish eyes, was seated in front of a large screen across which a line of figures was reeling at speed. She touched a knob and they went backwards. This seemed to satisfy her and she gave Charmian her attention.

'Mr Blood?'

'There hasn't been a Mr Blood for a long while,' said the young woman. 'Mr Dix is the manager.' Charmian observed with interest that behind this young woman was a large board from which were suspended bunches of keys, tagged and named.

At another desk, bare of any equipment except a green leather blotter, a bowl of flowers and a telephone, sat another young woman, smartly dressed in the uniform (blue suit and silk shirt) of a young executive. She too was a beauty. Bloods only employed young ladies with style.

Even as Charmian looked, a buzzer sounded from an inner room and the young woman rose and disappeared without a word. Master had called.

'And that was?' asked Charmian. 'I mean who's she?'

'Oh, that's Miss Yeoman, she's Mr Dix's assistant. But she's been working for Mr Eden a good deal the last few days.' The information was blandly delivered, but with meaning. 'Mr Dix has got Mr Eden in there now. He's the Managing Director of Homeline,' she said in answer to the question that Charmian hadn't asked. 'We've been seeing a lot of him lately. Changes, changes.' She went back to her screen, which was now sending up angry signals, with the air of one who might not be here at the end of the week and who won't mind if she is not. 'Mr Dix'll be sorry to keep you waiting.'

A group of three came through the door: first Miss Yeoman, and then, behind her, two dark-suited men, one in early middle age, and the other older, grey-haired and spectacled. He was doing the talking.

'That's the way of it, Leonard, we are between the Devil and the deep blue sea here. When I say that, then you have it in a nutshell. But we have several valuable properties in hand, and I would ask you to bear in mind that we deal with a better class of property than Ellistons or the L and N. We're handling Tinker's Grange and that is a very substantial affair, well in the million bracket, Len. And I may say we have had a nibble from royalty.'

Although Mr Dix called Mr Eden of Homeline by his given name, this did not seem to make them on familiar terms. Leonard Eden muttered something terse, ignored Charmian and took off, followed to the door by Miss Yeoman, who seemed to be receiving instructions at the door of the bright Mercedes. He rolled off, unscathed by any parking regulations.

As he always would be, Charmian concluded. One of life's success stories.

Mr Dix drew a breath. 'Thank God, he's gone. We've seen more of him lately than I want. Bring us some coffee, Mary, dear.'

Mary rose from her screen, which seemed the better without her as it steadied down and ceased the mild screams it had been sending out. 'So, are we still here?'

'As far as I know, dear, as far as I know.'

'And has the Queen enquired after Tinker's Grange?'

'Not to my knowledge, Mary,' said Mr Dix, growing more cheerful with every minute that parted him from Leonard Eden.

Then he saw Charmian, who had begun to think she was invisible. 'Selling or buying, miss?'

'This is Chief Superintendent Charmian Daniels,' said Mary, who appeared to know everything, secret or otherwise. 'Sorry, Miss Daniels, I heard you give a talk once. On women and crime. Riveted, I was.'

Miss Yeoman came back from the door which she had been holding open as the Mercedes disappeared from view. 'What lovely ties Mr Eden has,' she said. 'He's a lovely man.'

'Now you be careful,' called Mary. 'He's spoken for, he's a married man.'

Mr Dix's bonhomie disappeared to be replaced by gloom.

'Be quiet, you two. I can guess why you've come, Miss Daniels, it's about that poor young woman in Dulcet Road, isn't it?' He sighed. 'I think we've given one of your colleagues all the help we can.'

Charmian's eyes went to the board of keys. 'You have the keys to the house?'

'Yes. I was instructed by the owner to see that I always kept a set. She only rented, a short-term let. When the locks were replaced by the police I felt it right to get a set. They obliged.'

'Has your set remained here all the time?'

Mr Dix looked alert. 'What's up? Had a break-in? Nothing to do with us. We haven't handed them out, have we, Biddy?' He looked at Miss Yeoman. 'You're in charge of the keys.'

'Could anyone have taken a set without you knowing?'

'Well, they seem to be here still,' said Mr Dix, taking a look. 'So they would have to have come back as well. Biddy, what's your opinion? You're keeping quiet.'

Miss Yeoman took up a defensive position. 'As you know, I only returned from holiday the day before yesterday, and Mary has been in charge of the keys.'

'I had to go to the dentist,' said Mary blithely. 'I do the post too, you know. I've been in and out. I can't say I've been keeping an eye.' She stood up, dislodging several sets. 'Whoops, there they go. Hadham House and Crescent Place.'

Charmian prepared to leave Blood and Sons with the distinct impression that anyone who so wished could have taken and returned the keys to Dulcet Road. Although why they should then return the keys, having once removed them, puzzled her.

'Sorry we can't help you,' said Mr Dix as she retreated. 'But pleased to have met you, Chief Superintendent, and if you ever sell your house or desire another property, let us advise you. Or if you should wish to let your present home,' he added hopefully, 'we always have a list of American and overseas clients looking for good furnished accommodation near to Heathrow. Executives of important firms, diplomats, that sort of thing. Even the odd academic, but they are usually looking for the cheaper properties.'

He saw Charmian to the door, closing it behind her. She paused for a second on the threshold, then turned quickly back.

'What's a Chief Super doing on an enquiry like this?' Mr Dix was saying in an angry voice, by no means as polite as to Charmian. 'It's those cursed witches.' He saw Charmian.

'Just one question: Miss Charles had a lease. A short lease, I think you said. How short?'

'I'd have to consult the files.' Then as Charmian showed no sign of removing herself: 'A six months' lease.'

'Furnished then, I suppose?'

'A modicum of furniture.'

And she didn't provide any more, so she did not mean to stay. A convenience address for someone on the move. A bird of passage, this Miss Charles. If that really was her name.

'She must have provided references.'

'It would be in the file.'

'May I see it, please?'

The file was produced after the opening of several drawers which Charmian thought more for show than anything else. Mr Dix knew where he kept his files.

Unasked, she sat down to study it. Vivien Charles had paid her six months' rent in advance; she had provided no references other than her bank. The owner of the property was Barbour Rand Estates.

She closed the file. 'What was that about witches?'

'They advertise, Miss Daniels, they advertise. Look in the Post Office window. Or try the library. Good day to you.'

Charmian went straight to Merrywick Library, a place well known to her, and where a large display-board was open to all who wished to pin up a notice on payment of a small fee. She had used it once herself when Muff went missing. Muff could presumably read, or had friends who could, because she returned home at once.

There, amid the appeals for drivers for Help the Aged Club, and a notice of the next church bazaar in aid of the Merrywick and Slough Refuge for Battered Women, and another for Katherine Denzil's Dancing Class for Children – apply soon as there are still a few vacancies – (That's the chickenpox epidemic, thought Charmian knowledgeably, it weeded them out) there too was this large square notice, white on black, which made it stand out. It had been well placed in the middle of the board with the air of having elbowed out competition. Some careful hand had fixed four large drawing pins, so there was no danger of it getting dislodged.

TAROT READINGS

KNOW YOUR DREAMS: A GUIDE.

HEALTHY EATING.

And in smaller letters at the bottom: The Merrywick Guild of White Witches. There was a Slough telephone number.

Charmian removed the notice, taking it round to the librarian who was standing, in thought, behind her great desk.

'Why do you allow this to be put up?'

The librarian, Teresa Hawkes, took off her spectacles. 'You shouldn't have taken that down.' She stretched out her hand to regain the notice, but Charmian resisted.

'Don't you think it's dangerous?'

'Certainly not, it's quite harmless. They're nice women. I know them all. If you have a complaint, you should make it to our committee, Miss Daniels.'

She knew Charmian, they had crossed swords before. They usually stood on either side of a great divide on women's issues; Miss Hawkes was fiercely emotional, Charmian took a more intellectual approach, she liked evidence and a reasoned argument.

But now she was troubled, without much hard fact to go on.

'They are nice women, I'm sure, if you say so, Teresa. I haven't met them.' Although she intended to. 'But what they are doing could be dangerous.'

One of them was dead, after all. She had a feeling that a Pandora's Box had been opened and the furies were flying out.

She had enough sense of self-preservation not to show this too clearly before Teresa Hawkes's sceptical but interested gaze; she was enjoying their role reversal. It's quite shocking, her eyes were saying brightly, how prejudiced you can be on occasion. Charmian winced a little.

All the same, as she nervously flexed her right hand while walking towards Eton Bridge on her way home, Charmian was conscious of a rise of spirits, a sense of exhilaration. She was feeling better, she was really enjoying doing her own leg work.

Dolly had achieved this small miracle for her. 'God bless you, Dolly Barstow, for getting me into this.'

In Eton High Street, thinking, not for the first time, how odd it must be to live where every other shop was either an expensive restaurant or an equally expensive antique shop, she paused in front of one of the establishments she had just been deploring. This was an antique shop but of a dustier, humbler kind than the others. Very charming, though, and calling itself The Doll's House. In the window were a group of china-faced dolls dressed in Victorian clothes, with a bundle of worn-looking Teddy bears slumped behind them.

This shop also dealt in secondhand books, some in cases inside with a row of cheaper volumes stacked on a table in the street.

With interest, Charmian saw that another of those black cards advertising the services of the Merrywick Guild of White Witches was stuck on the window. It looked somewhat worn, as if it had been there for some time.

With even more interest did she observe that the astute

owner of The Doll's House had assembled a row of books on witchcraft for sale.

Montague Summers on *Witchcraft and Black Magic*, a battered paperback for 50p. Another by a different author, H. T. Rhodes, called *The Satanic Mass*, in better condition and costing 75p. She thought she recognised the author as the writer of several respectable textbooks on criminology seen in the library at Police College. So he might be reliable on witches. Did this row of books suggest a strong local interest? Were there not only witches in Merrywick, but also witches in Windsor, and sisters in Slough?

These two books were interesting, but what interested her more was a slim hardback, published by the Python Press, entitled *The Earth Goddess and Her Lore: For modern followers of the ancient faith*. The author was Alice Peacock of Merrywick.

Charmian went inside and bought all three books, tucking them under her arm to read when she reached home. A car stopped beside her and Dolly's voice said: 'Hello. Shopping?'

'Look,' Charmian displayed her purchases. 'I've been supporting a local industry.'

'Alice Peacock? I believe she publishes them herself. She is the Python Press; her father left her a small printing business and she has turned it into something else.'

Two college boys strolled past, aloof, silent, lordly but dishevelled. Perhaps it was the fashionable way to look. Charmian moved aside, feeling that the world would always move aside for them. Such self-confidence, not a bad way to grow up.

Dolly poked her head out of the car again. 'I was looking for you. Come and eat in that wine bar across the road and talk.'

The Prince Harry Wine Bar had once been a dairy and bore witness to that still in the flagged stone floor and the green and white tiles on the walls which the present owner, an old Etonian called Harry Trefusis, had chosen to leave *in situ*. Indeed, he dressed up to it, wearing an old-style milkman's blue striped apron and a straw hat. The purists said that this was what fishmongers had once worn (and still did wear, if you shopped in the right places) but Harry knew what his customers liked. A bit of style.

He waved his hand at Dolly whom he knew of old. 'Hi.'

'Come here often?' asked Charmian.

'Now and again. But Harry and I were at university together. Then he went into wine and I went into the police. I have more of a career structure and I'll have a pension, but he's richer.' At the moment her career prospects did not seem to be cheering her up. 'They have quite a nice Beaujolais here, and the lasagne's not bad.'

'Let's have that, then.'

'I'd better only have a glass, I've got to work this afternoon.'

'What's up, Dolly?'

Dolly looked a bit sick, but she just shrugged. 'Try the wine, not bad is it?' Then over the lasagne, she said, 'Had the medical report on Vivien Charles: the post mortem. I saw the doc. She was pregnant.'

'Ah.' Charmian put down her fork.

Dolly pushed the food around on her plate, turning her head away and looking out of the window. 'Got an old Scotch pathologist. Glasgow chap. I expect you know him?'

'Fordyce?'

'That's right. He told me himself. Three months or so gone, he said. Then he said, "Poor lass, she'd never have come to term, the embryo was all wrong. A strange little manikin, it would have been."'

Dolly looked at Charmian. 'I don't think he should have said that, do you? But I don't think he could stop himself. It just popped out.'

The two women sat in silence, the food untasted. Dolly drained her wine.

'She wouldn't have known.'

'About the malformation? No, of course not. I wonder who the father was?'

'That's something we'll have to look into.'

'You could ask the witch ladies. See if they know.'

'That is something I positively do not wish to do, but I can see I will have to.'

They ate in silence for a while, then Charmian said, 'I'd like to meet them. As a group.'

'I can arrange that.' Dolly got up. She took the bill. 'Let me do this. You're helping me. And Father and Elman are looking the other way while we do it. They've agreed.'

Dolly consulted with the waitress, collected her change, handed over a tip, then returned to the table to pick up her coat. She put her bag and the bill on the table while she did so. Charmian got the impression that she would've liked to have said something more, but nothing came out.

'Goodbye. I'll be in touch.'

She walked off, manifestly in low spirits, leaving Charmian to consider it all.

'Poor Dolly, she's in deep,' thought Charmian. 'Doesn't like what she might learn about the parentage of the baby.' Mr Fox?

But wasn't that what the warlock always did? Impregnate the witch.

She felt sorry for Dolly Barstow, but there were mixed feelings. She lifted her right hand and pulled at the fingers, they felt all right, quite normal, they *were* normal, just unwilling to pick up a pen and do some writing. It was all in the mind, of course, and that was bad, but she had to admit that she was passionately interested in the problem of Vivien Charles, which she might, jokingly, say she had in hand.

She drew towards her the bill that Dolly had paid and absently left behind, and started to make notes with her left hand. It worked quite well.

Never let your right hand know what your left hand is doing.

Chapter Four

Charmian walked over the bridge to her home, while Dolly drove back to her official duties. The bridge across the Thames between Windsor and Eton is for pedestrians only and in summer is crowded with visitors enjoying the view of the river and the houses that line it.

Charmian pushed her way through a group of Japanese tourists who seemed to have got lost. In the distance, towards the castle, their woman guide was waving a red umbrella to attract their attention. She failed and as Charmian passed them, the group seemed to take a communal decision to walk towards Eton, leaving their guide to run after them. 'St George's Chapel,' she was calling. 'Now it is the Chapel we go to see. After that the College.' The wind carried her voice away.

In the hall of her house in Maid of Honour Row, Charmian saw Muff sitting on a suitcase of expensive, striped leather which Charmian knew to come from Loewes. Only one person in her life owned luggage as expensive as that collection. She also smelt coffee, and mixed with it a floral Italian scent she recognised.

'Kate?'

A tall, tanned girl wearing jeans and a cotton shirt appeared. Ralph Laurens, thought Charmian, who had learnt to detect expensive clothes, even sometimes to buy them.

'Hi, Godmother.'

'So, you're back.'

'As you see. Delhi could no longer hold me.'

And, of course, your mother, Annie, my best friend, did

not say: Come home, Charmian is in trouble? But she did not utter this aloud. As with so much in her life, it went unexpressed. Possibly this was what her hand resented.

'Where's Joe?'

Joe was the young man with whom Kate had started her journey. There was usually a young man. Either she started out with one or she came back with one, rarely the same lad. But Joe had seemed serious.

'Oh, I lost him,' said Kate airily. 'He fell in with a lovely young *begum* and stayed on to help her with her stables. She breeds Arabians.'

Her godmother could see that Kate had not enjoyed being pushed aside, even for a stable of true-bred Arabs.

'You should have stayed yourself.'

'Not me.' Kate poured a mug of coffee for Charmian. 'Anyway, it was time for home. I'd got all I could out of Lutyens. A great man, though.'

In Charmian's possibly prejudiced opinion (because she loved the girl), Kate would one day be a good architect, possibly even a great one, but she had a lot of things to work through yet, with, unluckily for her if you looked at it that way, the money to take her time. But she was a warm, affectionate goddaughter, whose occasional spells of lodging with Charmian were appreciated.

'Seen your parents?'

Annie and Jack Cooper were old friends of Charmian who lived in Windsor in a marriage whose battles gave alarm to their friends but apparently some pleasure to the married pair. They parted and came together again like performers in a dance.

'Not yet. Haven't been back long enough. Have to prepare myself. What's the position at the moment? Under one roof?'

'As far as I know,' said Charmian cautiously.

'Been quite a spell this time. How's Annie's work doing?'

Annie was a well-known artist, much praised but sometimes lazy. The money which emancipated her and Kate was inherited.

'Got an exhibition planned for the Hardcastle Gallery.'

The Hardcastle was a smart Bond Street gallery sited in a minute shop between two famous jewellers. You were in the money if your work sold there.

'Thought she despised it.' Bond Street Boys, Annie had called them.

'She does. But they made her an offer.'

Annie had a shrewd business head, without doubt she had struck a hard bargain.

'And what's your big interest at the moment, Godmother? You're usually getting some study together: criminous women, delinquent kids . . . What is it this time?'

'Don't you patronise me, child.'

'Sorry, Godmother.'

'As it happens I have got something . . . Women and Witchcraft.'

Kate opened her eyes wide. 'In history or in literature?'

'In the present.'

'Do you really mean it? Where? I must meet them.'

'There's a group of women in Merrywick calling themselves white witches.'

'Oh, they're good,' said Kate at once. 'Earth mothers, white magic, that sort of thing.'

'One of them has been murdered.'

Kate said accusingly, 'I think you're enjoying yourself.'

'In a way.'

Muff came in through the window, looking neither to right nor left, but leaping straight for Kate.

Kate hugged her. 'A real witch's cat, you.'

'Thanks. I'll remember that.'

'I suppose you've called on old Mother Peacock?'

'You mean you know about her?'

'Oh, darling, yes. She's famous. Dad went to her for warts once. Disappeared like magic. He thought it was magic. Don't say she's been done in?'

'No.'

'Or murdered anyone? I can't believe that.'

Charmian did not answer. It was possible, anything was possible.

'A young woman called Vivien Charles was found dead in her own house. I don't think you'd have known her, Kate.'

Kate, whose own history was not without violence, left the subject alone. 'Let me know if I can do anything, Godmother.'

When Kate had gone upstairs to unpack, taking a purring Muff with her, Charmian collected her thoughts. They were far from clear, which irritated her, since she prided herself on being a clear-minded person.

I am interested in women's groupings. Why do women come together? Is there something specific to their sex in any one such group?

Crime can draw women together. Two years ago I examined one such group which came together to commit a felony, but they were just women who happened to be criminals. They were barely friends, and yet they were companions.

Although I said that about friendship, imbedded in these groups there is usually one close relationship, although the women concerned may not even like each other very much.

So I think women form groups if there is a strong personal relationship somewhere. The Queen Bee principle?

Then why have this little group, who call themselves white witches, come together? They are believers. Women as believers? Is that my subject? But there has to be one strong believer among them to whom the others hold. I suppose I ought to try to identify her.

A telephone call from Dolly Barstow broke into her thoughts.

Dolly was in a hurry, but she got her message across: A meeting this afternoon of the Merrywick witches. They would all be there. She would do the driving.

Leaving Kate to settle her possessions, of which she had a great many, all important to her, Charmian telephoned a young doctor, now a GP in practice in Richmond, whom she had got to know in an earlier investigation. He had been a swain of Dolly Barstow's but they had floated apart and he

47

was now married to a pretty girl who bred Dalmatians.

'Hello, Len.'

Dr Lennard (Christian name Alwyn, but he liked to be called Len) answered cautiously; he recognised the speaker's voice, and in his experience of Charmian Daniels, trouble came with her.

'I didn't think I'd get you. Thought you'd be out seeing patients.'

'Just having a cup of tea.'

There was a light, falsetto growl in the background. 'Down, Lucifer. Sorry, Charmian, just one of the dogs, likes a saucer of tea. What can I do for you?' Nothing, I hope, he was saying inside himself, but contact with Charmian inspired a certain desire to co-operate even in a blameless GP. What effect she must have on those with a crime on their conscience wasn't worth thinking about.

'Professional advice.'

This was a dread question. 'Not ill, are you?' he said with apprehension.

'Just a few obstetric questions.'

Good heavens, he thought, surely not?

'Not for me.' He could hear the gurgle of amusement in Charmian's voice; damn her, she always had laughed at him. So had Dolly Barstow, which had annoyed him because he was a serious person. 'Professional need to know.'

'Can't you get one of your own lot to do it for you? I daresay you will check on what I might say anyway.'

'Oh, come on, off the cuff and quickly. I want to know what factors make an embryo go wrong.'

'What a question! Do you hear a hollow laugh? It needs a book to answer. Anything, many things. Genetics, some drugs, alcohol occasionally, if you take too much of it, a fever, or just bad luck. Usually the latter. Of course, a lot of women never find out, they just miscarry so early they may not have known they were pregnant. I suppose I mustn't ask why you need to know?'

'Just a case.' Charmian was evasive. 'I may be able to

tell you later. Does the father contribute anything to this mischance?'

'His genetic material might,' agreed Len. 'Some people are just incompatible.'

'Could a shock do it?'

'Probably. Did she have a shock?'

'I'm beginning to think she might have done.'

There had already been, as Charmian was to discover, a meeting of the Merrywick Guild of White Witches, summoned by Miss Peacock, after a short consultation with Miss Winnie Eagle, but held in Caprice Dash's shop in Slough.

Birdie Peacock arrived well ahead of the others. 'How's business, Caprice?' Birdie had a stake in the shop. The group had really grown up around Birdie and her many interests in the spiritual world.

'Not bad, not bad at all. Summer's always a slow time, we shall do better as autumn comes on. It's the dark evenings and the smell of wood-smoke.' There was a poet hidden away inside Caprice, the retailer witch. 'People are drawn to our sort of thing then.'

'What about postal orders?' Twickers had a large postal trade.

'Ah, there we are up. Well up.'

'So the ad in *The Times* got results?' said Miss Peacock with satisfaction.

'I believe it's the one in *The Guardian* that's been the draw. I think the readers are more open-minded.'

'And what are the best sellers?'

Caprice considered. 'The dowsing equipment does well. I expect they are after finding hidden treasure. Quite a run on crystal balls, although I never find them very satisfactory myself, I haven't the knack. Magic holographs are down, they're more Christmassy, I think. I've had a lot of enquiries about the bio-rhythm tapes. Incense and oils, likewise. I think ageing yuppies burn them at dinner parties and feel clever, not a serious use at all.'

'And the black wax manikins? I don't see any in the shop. Don't say they were sold?'

'One or two, but they're really not our style. Nasty I think and so do the customers, even those looking for a joke. So I've put them in the back stockroom. I may shift them at Hallowe'en.'

'Where did you order them from?'

'A voodoo wholesaler that I've often dealt with. His goods usually have such style, but he's let me down this time. The specimen I ordered from was nothing like the ones he sent. I think he's got a new manufacturer.'

The manikins were made, as she shrewdly guessed, in a small back room in Hackney where the dealer's eldest son improvised whatever took his fancy. This last season, his fancy had turned darker, become sombre and violent.

Birdie Peacock took a look at the shelves. 'I see Lavarack is going well. I haven't tried that myself.'

'Don't, dear, it's most unpleasant. But the honey and seaweed preserve is tastier than you might think. Nutritious as well.' Caprice knew how to promote her wares and on occasion this commercial side irritated her friend and patron.

Birdie reacted now. 'We must never forget we are a craft, and a very ancient one. We owe it to our fellow women.'

Caprice was less dedicated than Birdie, more of a sales-woman. She had inherited her premises from her father who had been a grocer. But there was no place for good old-fashioned grocer shops in an area devoted to the super-market, so Caprice had turned first to so-called health foods and natural remedies. But even in this field she faced sharp competition, so she had moved on, by a natural progression somehow, to being what she was now: the purveyor of magic and mystery and weird toys. On the way, the witchcraft bit had been added to her. As if by magic, she told herself, on awaking one morning after a supper with Birdie to find she had been declared a natural witch. 'The best sort,' Birdie had said. 'Not many like you. I was lucky to find you.'

The revelation had come to Birdie in a dream after their supper, not unconnected, some might say, with the curry that they had eaten and the fact that Caprice had a shop that needed support.

At the moment Caprice felt a double person: one pair of hands selling and another raising spells – which never seemed to work although Birdie said they did. All she knew was that whenever she tried a spell on a particular enemy (Caprice always had an enemy or two around) they seemed to do better than ever. Possibly she hadn't quite mastered the knack of malediction.

Her two personalities could be united by the use of alcohol, but she kept this from Birdie and the other wiccers. They called themselves this on occasion, from the old English word Wicca for witch, pronouncing the two cs hard, although more properly soft. Hence the name of her shop: Twickers. It had been called William Dash, Grocer.

'I don't know how the murder of poor Viv will touch us. Can't do us any good.' Her tone was unemotional, she hadn't, as it happened, had a lot of time for Vivien Charles.

All the women had been questioned by a plain-clothes detective, Dolly keeping well out of the way, although sensed as a presence in the undergrowth.

'It's a horrible business,' said Miss Peacock. 'I didn't know anything useful, but naturally I did what I could.'

'Nothing to do with us, but, the trouble is, with those objects laid out round the body it looks as though it is.' Caprice had made it her business to find out as much as she could about the circumstances of Vivien's death, and although nothing had been reported in detail in the papers she had her own channels of information. 'But they were all wrong, not genuine at all.' A mistake, she thought, which might cost the killer dear. Mistakes of that sort always did in her experience.

'We know that, but who else does?'

The two women were silent. Then Alice Peacock said, 'I explained to the detective who spoke to me that our intent was wholly good, and that . . . that muck was the kind of perversity we would have nothing to do with. I don't know if he believed me.'

'Could you expect him to? Probably got images of a black mass and naked bodies in his mind.'

'I thought Dolly Barstow might have spoken up for us.'

'Probably ashamed of knowing us.'

The shopbell rang, announcing the arrival of Miss Eagle and Mrs Flight, an occasional member of the group, now rounded up and brought in by Miss Eagle in spite of her protests that she should really be playing bridge.

'I know you'd rather forget you're one of us, Jean, but you owe to us as women to come.'

'Thank God my Fred is dead.'

'He knows all about it and approves,' said Miss Eagle firmly.

Jean Flight had joined the group in order to get in touch with her late husband, which she had done satisfactorily.

Winifred Eagle had been christened in the Church of England in the straightforward way and for some years had worshipped at St Jerome's Church in Merrywick, but she had never felt at home. She had tried Methodism, a charismatic church, Yoga and Zen and had even made an attempt to be a Quaker but had not been encouraged.

Then a visit to Avebury had provided her with an 'experience'. Birdie had been on the tour as well and the realisation of what they had felt there, the strong sense of a female presence coming through the earth and woodland, of a tug in their guts as a wand of ash had moved in Birdie's hands, of their being one with it, all had been very strong.

Led, was how they put it. Birdie was already practised in Tarot and had some success with the crystal ball.

Caprice had brought commercialism with her. At the same time, although Birdie regarded herself as their leader, Caprice had made them more of a group by means of her shop, which gave them a focus and a corporate identity.

They were all women who had the leisure to meet in the afternoon as well as in the evening, and, of course, they belonged to other associations, too. Birdie was keen on the Women's Institute and was secretary this year of her local group; Winifred Eagle was an active member of the Cats' Club, Slough and Windsor Branch, and usually had a resident deprived cat with her as well as her own black angel. Even Caprice found time to take lessons in bridge once a week to improve her bidding.

But what bound them all together was that they were all believers who wanted to find faith in something, but had not succeeded in meeting their needs in a more orthodox way. Closet feminists, to believe in an Earth Mother and a Great Goddess suited them.

The Tarot Cards had brought in Vivien Charles who seemed, as Birdie said, a restless, dissatisfied soul. Birdie had never revealed what she saw in the Tarot Cards for Vivien, that was a professional matter about which one did not talk, but it cannot have been good.

Under Caprice's care they had advertised, made a local name for themselves, earned a little money – none of them was averse to that – and enjoyed some publicity. It was enjoyable to be interviewed by the local newspaper and talk about natural cures on Eton Radio. Some of their neighbours looked askance, but on the whole the group did not mind, conscious as they were of doing good things, like curing warts, alleviating acne, soothing arthritis and calling back lost animals.

Caprice had brought in Josh Fox. He had come into her shop one day and somehow got an invitation out of her over a drink of whisky. They had welcomed his interest, no doubt about that; he was an attractive man: like the young Olivier, Birdie had once said in an unguarded moment. And although Caprice had laughingly called him their warlock or male wiccer, that was not what he was. Warlocks had a definite function and Josh had never so much as touched one of them.

Sexless, the relationship with wiccers and putative warlock might be, but there was no denying that the band had been less harmonious since he arrived, as they competed for his attention.

They gathered for coffee in the stockroom at the back, surrounded by boxes of mystery puzzles, Monsters in Mazes (described wrongly by Birdie who had never really looked at it, as a kind of Snakes and Ladders game, and who had given one as a birthday present to a small neighbour, much to the alarm of his single-parent mother), tins, jars and cartons of herbs and potions, some in capsules, others in hard pills. Nostrums of all sorts were sold by Caprice who put a good mark-up on each item. Magic did not come free.

Caprice had once made a collection of African witch-doctor masks, thinking they might make good window dressing, but they had proved so baleful that they clashed with the Good Earth Mother image she was promoting, so she had banished them to the back where they gazed with empty eyes on her friends.

Caprice disliked them now, they were fakes, she had been cheated by the little Pakistani who had sold them to her. She had put a curse on him, but he had survived unscathed. Indeed, to prosper, with a new red and silver French car, customised with golden wreaths of flowers on the panels. Either spells did not work in Slough or she had got the wrong one. It might be the climate, you probably needed more sun or a higher temperature, and although she had put her ingredients in the microwave that had not helped either, though it had created a nasty smell.

Birdie turned the mask hanging behind her chair to face the wall. 'Rather not have it looking at me.' She stood up and smoothed her skirt. 'Shall we start with a short prayer to the Great Mother?'

Winifred Eagle was fidgety and ill at ease tonight, anxious to get on with things. She was worried about her black cat who was missing. 'I don't sense She's here tonight somehow. There isn't the feeling.'

'Faith is not feeling,' said Birdie with severity. She was a true believer.

Caprice said, 'Prayers or not, I think we should talk

54

things over before the two policewomen get here. Work out what we are going to say.'

'The truth,' said Birdie.

'There are truths and truths.'

'Poor Vivien, poor child,' said Winifred Eagle.

Mrs Flight kept silent, she was a relative newcomer and not anxious to involve herself with the ruling body of the group. She sipped her coffee, which was bitterer than ever tonight. No one, she reflected sadly, had ever taught Caprice to cook.

Birdie allowed herself a few moments of private devotion to the Earth Goddess, who in her mind's eye bore a decided resemblance to Birdie herself, only larger and younger. A pleasing sense of divinity descended upon her.

The Goddess told her what to say. 'You introduced Vivien to us, Caprice, so perhaps you should start.'

'I didn't introduce her. She came into the shop to get a Tarot reading, which you gave her, Birdie.'

'She was a troubled soul.'

'And how right she was,' said Winifred Eagle sadly. 'Poor child, poor child, I liked her so much, although she wasn't normally the sort of girl I get to know. Chance brings strange companions together.'

'I always had the feeling,' said Mrs Flight, 'that she didn't come by chance, that she knew what she was doing.'

No one listened to her, which was usually her fate.

'What's happened to those two women?' said Caprice, breaking across Mrs Flight. 'They're late.'

'So what are we hoping to get out of this meeting?' Dolly asked, turning the car in the direction of Slough. 'By the way, we're meeting in the shop in Slough, and we're running late.' As she drove, she said, 'And the reason I'm late is something came up . . . I've been offered, or nearly offered, I can have it if I want, a job as a kind of co-ordinator of crimes against women and children. Promotion, of course. But I don't know whether to go for it or not.'

'Sounds as if it might be a kind of side-alley.' Leading

nowhere much. Charmian had been offered jobs of that kind herself in the past and turned them down.

'Yes, you have to recognise the signs, don't you? I've said I'll think about it. The offer remains open.' She steered the car expertly through the crowded traffic lanes. 'I've got plenty of other things to think about. We've traced Vivien Charles's father, her only remaining relation. Her mother died about ten years ago. He remarried and has more or less lost touch with Vivien. That is, she kept up, the odd letter and telephone call, but never told him much. He knew she'd moved to an address in Merrywick – she used to live in Ealing – but didn't know why. He assumed she must have a job here.'

'But she didn't have.'

'No, but he knew she'd had a small inheritance from an aunt and she'd said something about "finding herself". If he thought about it, and I don't believe he did, he thought she was doing that in Merrywick.'

'With the Witches of Merrywick?'

'They seem to have been her only contact. She doesn't appear to have had any other friends; she only had a short-term lease on the house and it doesn't look as if she was staying.'

'Someone made her pregnant. Where did she work before she came here? She had a job?'

'Her dad thinks it was with a wine merchants at first, then she moved to a bigger outfit in Hatton Woods – we haven't located it yet but we will. And, of course, no letters or addresses round her house. It's inconceivable a girl of that age didn't have a life somewhere – friends, places that knew her, where she bought clothes or had her hair done – but by God there's no trace of it. It's as if she deliberately drew a line through her old life.'

Charmian looked out of the window as the car turned off Slough High Street, crowded with shoppers going in and out of the supermarkets and multiple stores, into the quieter Havant Way. Dolly would learn. There are always two stories to be told. While you are trying to put one together, there is another one underneath that demands to be heard.

'You'll find Twickers interesting. Caprice has really put it together. Interesting without being mad, if you see what I mean.'

'Did you ever shop there?'

'Of course,' said Dolly with a grin. 'Couldn't resist. Bought myself some Burning Oil. I was supposed to get visions in the smoke, but I didn't see anything. Caprice said it was old stock and marked down in price.'

'I shall be watching out for Caprice.'

'Oh, she's an entrepreneur all right. She's got the touch. Birdie thinks it's all her, but Caprice is really the Queen Bee. I sussed that out after two meetings: she was watching me watching her.'

Both women felt they had walked into a circle of eyes when they arrived at Twickers. Caprice led them into the back room.

Caprice was a tall, well-built woman, with broad shoulders and muscular hands; she seemed as though she could look after herself. A little careful eccentricity appeared in her clothes, nothing too homespun, but a flowing cotton skirt of gypsy colours and rows of amber and coloured beads.

She had greeted Dolly with a smile, apparently quite relaxed and pleased to see her. Charmian got a stiffer handshake. 'We're all here, ready and waiting.'

One new arrival had got there before them: Joshua Fox.

As soon as she saw him and was introduced, Charmian felt sure that was not his real name. He didn't react to it in the right way, no sense of possessiveness, instead a sub-terranean surprise as if he hadn't been called that when he left home. Wherever home was.

A sinewy, tough fellow with a sweep of shining black hair, and younger than she had expected. The right age for Dolly. But not if he thought he was a warlock.

He did not strike her in any way as being obsessed, or mad, or magical, but he was certainly possessed of remark-able magnetism. She could see why the ladies were happy they had captured him. For herself, a sort of anger allied to fear, which she recognised as coming from her near rape, swept over. She repressed it quickly, turning to one of the women.

She recognised her neighbour. 'Hello, Miss Eagle, how's the cat?'

'I'm worried about him.'

'Winifred is always worried about her cat.' Caprice poured them red wine in metal goblets. She had produced the wine and she was burning something sweet and aromatic in a bowl. Candles had been lit in pewter holders – silver would have been more correct but Caprice could not run to the expense, and pewter was very mediaeval.

All the women were reacting to Joshua ('Call me Josh'), Dolly included, sex appeal like that always had its effect. Even Charmian's own reaction meant something.

'It's rough about Viv.' He had a deep, sweet voice, with a speech pattern of neat vowels and clean consonants. A trained voice? Charmian asked herself, wondering if he was an actor.

'That's why we're here,' said Dolly.

Caprice took up the challenge. 'Is this official, or are we meeting as friends?'

'I think it has to be regarded as official. Sorry.'

'I don't think you are. I think it's what you came for in the first place: to check us over.'

Dolly was silent.

'Crime prevention, it's called, isn't it? Only we're not criminals.'

Dolly still said nothing.

'I could cast your horoscope and tell you where you were going,' said Caprice with some vindictiveness.

Birdie tried to restore the balance. 'I think we owe it to our sister Vivien to do what we can. She was a good child. Ignorant but learning.'

'What were you teaching her?' asked Charmian.

'Nothing wrong,' said Birdie seriously. 'How to worship, how to love the world and the earth, our Mother.'

'She was three months' pregnant. Do you know who was her lover?'

There was silence.

'Did she say anything to you about it?'

'No.' Birdie shook her head. She pulled herself together after what had been a shock. 'But I am not against fruitfulness nor is our Great Mother.'

'It takes two,' said Dolly. 'She didn't do it on her own. Any ideas? What about you, Josh?'

He took up the loaded question with coolness: 'I'm just an observer here. Saw the advertisement and thought I'd look in. And I've always been interested. Some of the things here seemed to work. Or I thought so. Faith healing, maybe, but it got rid of a nasty go of migraine I had. Then I had a look in the crystal ball and saw a scene from life, won't say what, but it meant something to me.'

'I shall ask you about that later,' said Charmian.

He shrugged. 'Might have been hallucination. Or mild hypnosis. Some of Miss Peacock's prayers do tend that way.'

'Are you a teacher, Mr Fox?' I'm not calling him Josh, too cosy altogether.

'No, why?'

'You talk like one.'

'I'm a writer. Freelance.'

'Published?'

'This is hostile.' He sat back, with an annoying half-smile on his face.

It was, Charmian admitted. We'll get to the bottom of you, Mr Fox. Check your address. Find out if you really live there, which I doubt. Find out who you are.

The black masks on the walls with glass balls for eyes glinted in the light. Caprice's burning herbs got up her nose, and together with the heat of the candles made Charmian feel dizzy.

Dolly had gone quiet. In a dark distance, Charmian heard Birdie's voice: 'Shall we say a prayer for our sister?' Life seemed to be sucked out of the air.

Charmian drew her energies together. 'This isn't a church service, Miss Peacock, but an investigation.' I wish I was sure of that, she thought.

She went to the door and threw it open. A cold wind blew through. She took charge. Well, it felt like that. Dolly didn't seem disposed to.

'One thing Sergeant Barstow hasn't told you: you will all be asked to give blood samples. Also certain forensic samples: from your clothes, possibly from your houses.'

'Can we refuse?' asked Caprice. There was a mutter from the others.

Josh Fox did not ask, Charmian noticed.

As they drove away, Charmian said, 'Call yourself Sergeant Barstow to them in future, Dolly.'

It was her warning.

Dolly received it with a silent nod. It made good sense.

'Can we go back to something earlier? The house in Dulcet Road was entered when it was supposed to be locked up. That's one thing to clear up. But earlier, the door to the house was left unlocked which was how Mrs Flaxon got in. Who left it unlocked?'

'The killer? Going off in a panic?'

'Could be. But perhaps there was another caller. What about Forensics?'

Dolly shrugged. 'I'll see what they can suggest.' But she didn't have high hopes.

Chapter Five

Denise Flaxon let herself into her flat in Slough. It was empty. It was always empty. It felt empty even when she was in it.

This was early evening after the day on which Charmian and Dolly Barstow had attended the meeting in Caprice's shop. Denise had driven past the shop while the meeting was going on without knowing of the meeting or even noticing Twickers.

It was a week to the day that she had found Vivien Charles dead. Not a pleasant thought, and one that Denise put to the bottom of the file of all the other thoughts that worried her.

Today had not been a good one at Elysium Creams. A meeting of franchise holders had been called by the area manager, at which their sales figures had been reviewed. Denise's had not been good. Low. In fact, the lowest of all the franchisees, except for little Mrs Harries who was six months' pregnant and from whom not much could be expected at the moment. Denise had got the distinct impression that the area manager thought Denise was not trying. You might think this would not matter to Elysium Creams because Denise's franchise was bought and paid for by her and what she did not sell was her own business. (Or lack of it.) But what you did not sell, you did not buy from the main stocks and that did matter to Elysium Creams. Was, indeed, their main motive for creating franchises.

'Come now, Denise, dear,' he had said in front of everyone, 'you can do better than this. You did do better when you started with us. When did you take up your franchise now? Four months ago, was it?'

'Three,' said Denise.

'One of our brightest salespersons, I said so myself when you joined the team. Said it aloud, didn't I? And so you were for a couple of months. What's gone wrong, dear?'

Naturally Denise could not answer that. Bloody fool, she thought, but keeping the soft puzzled look on her face the meanwhile, as if she was as perplexed as he was.

'You've got one of our best areas there in Merrywick, bristling with opportunity. I said so when I let you have it, didn't I?'

Denise admitted that he had and implied she would try harder. Work her patch more efficiently. But from the way the rest of the flock eyed her, she got the impression that when her present franchise ran out, it would not be renewed. Elysium reserved to themselves the right to hold back a contract. Made sense when you thought about it.

Mrs Harries leaned across her ample middle, as far as she could lean, that was, and patted Denise's hand. 'Don't worry, love, he always goes on like this. I've heard it all before. He always picks on someone. Just you this time.'

Denise tried to look as if she cared. But the episode had tired her and she was glad to get back to her private emptiness at Oaktree House, Woodstock Close, although it was not an apartment she looked upon with relish as a rule or thought of as home.

Home was where? Where you thought it was, and she did not know what to think. She felt homeless.

No post, but a free newspaper on the mat and milk in the fridge. She started to make a cup of tea.

As expected the newspaper headlined the murder in Merrywick. You couldn't expect them to pass over the local sensation, but she was very grateful that her name was not mentioned although her discovery of the body was described. The police had said they would do their best to keep her name out of it.

Denise went through to the kitchen and made a pot of

62

tea. She was thirsty but not hungry, she never was hungry these days, which was just as well because her refrigerator contained nothing but a dried old lemon and a carton of LongLife milk. She would go out in a little while and buy some food for a meal in the local supermarket which kept late hours.

She kicked off her shoes, they were higher of heel than the ones she usually wore, not really her style, but right for the job. If you were selling beauty products then you had need to look elegant and feminine.

She sipped her tea. She would have to go to the inquest, of course, but she thought she could manage that, and the young policewoman (what a job for a woman, Denise could not admire it) had promised her it would be a formality as far as she was concerned. It was a great pity she had found the body, it ought to have been somebody else.

Someone else had been there. The door was unlocked. Vivien hadn't got up and turned the key, and then arranged herself again on the floor.

Her tea was too hot, so Denise poured in some more milk. Perhaps it had been the milkman who had called in Dulcet Road? Opening the door to leave a pint of milk, then seeing Vivien and running away. But no, black joke. It had not been the milkman. She was as sure as anyone could be that it had not been the milkman, nor the postman, nor a boy delivering a parcel from a shop.

She couldn't be certain that the police had taken in the significance of the unlocked door through which she herself had got in. They might have thought that the killer left the door open behind him. To Denise this seemed most unlikely and she had to recognise that the young police sergeant might think this, too.

In which case she would be wondering who had dropped in, and be looking for him.

That made two of them. Because Denise was wondering and looking as well.

It had occurred to her that she might be in danger herself. She tried to dismiss this thought as a transferred anxiety.

After all, she had plenty of things to worry about, including the inquest, but somehow the thought of that unlocked door nagged away. Could anyone have been watching her? Perhaps been watching the house?

She finished her tea, then stood up to study her reflection in the wall mirror – one of the few decorations, if that was what it was, that she had added to the flat. But after all, a woman had to know what she looked like.

'This murder is nothing to do with Mrs Flaxon,' she told her reflection. 'Stop kicking yourself around.'

A dark curl had got disarranged, she was about to do something to it when her doorbell rang.

Some people like callers and look forward to them, Denise Flaxon did not. She was in the state of preferring solitude, and her experience in Dulcet Road (even if she had brought it on herself and it was her own fault) reinforced this feeling.

'Standoffish,' was how Flo Jessamon, her neighbour in the flat below, dubbed her.

But it did not stop Miss Jessamon ringing the doorbell. One did one's duty, even to an unfriendly neighbour. 'I should never forgive myself if any harm came to her through any neglect of mine,' she said to herself, ignoring the fact that she was passionately keen to get a look inside Mrs Flaxon's rooms. Some people collect stamps, pictures, secondhand books or china pot lids with pictures on, but Flo Jessamon collected interiors. Of other people's houses. It was a higher form of nosiness.

She smiled hopefully as the door was opened. 'I don't want to disturb you, Mrs Flaxon.' She passed over the expression on Mrs Flaxon's face which said she was doing exactly that. 'I just wanted to have a word with you. I'm Miss Jessamon from the floor below.'

'I know.' It was not a promising opening. We finish here, it seemed to state.

Flo removed her smile and said with gravity, 'I don't want to alarm you, but I thought I ought to speak.'

'What about?'

Denise was not aware of letting Miss Jessamon in, but somehow she was there inside and they were both standing in the sitting room. Other contacts of Miss Jessamon had observed the same phenomenon. It was something akin to the Indian Rope trick – Miss Jessamon's father was known to have served with the army in India – a Now you see her, Now you don't kind of thing, hard to reconcile with Miss Jessamon's small but sturdy frame.

'I wouldn't fuss, I'm not a fusser,' began Flo. Mrs Flaxon's living room was a disappointment to her. A quick glance told her that nothing had been done since the last tenant, a Mr Burges, who had not himself been a homemaker of merit. It was clean, it was tidy, but that was about all you could say. Mr Burges had not even been that. 'If it wasn't for this nasty murder so close . . . Merrywick isn't far . . . You've heard about the murder, I suppose?' Must have done, she could see the local paper on the table, and with her long sight could read it as well.

'I don't want to think about it.' The words popped out before Denise could stop them.

Flo was deeply, if falsely, sympathetic. 'I know. One doesn't. So terrible. But one can't bury one's head, can one?' Something Flo was never likely to do, her eyes were always brightly peeping about. 'And this man has been seen hanging about outside. I thought I ought to tell you.'

'What man?'

'The one that's been lurking around the house.' A couple of dusty urban trees stood in the road just by the block of flats; it was possible to lurk in them. Just possible.

'What sort of man? What's he like?'

'I don't know. I haven't seen him myself,' said Flo regretfully. 'But Mr Schmidt on the ground floor said he was a very ordinary sort of man.' But then anyone might seem ordinary to Mr Schmidt, who for fifty years now had been so far from ordinary himself, having lived, as he would say through so many horrors in Germany during the war that only a good wife and a sound digestion had brought him through. However, his wife had whispered to Flo that, except for the short sojourn on the Isle of Man, he had spent the whole of the war in Manchester writing crime stories. So which was true? But wherever truth lay it made Mr Schmidt himself not one of your common, run-of-the-mill types.

'It seems most unlikely he had anything to do with the murder, whoever he is.'

'But we ought to be on our guard.'

'That killer must be far away by now.'

'Unless he lives locally. We know murderers often observe their victims before striking. I for one don't want to be raped or murdered in my bed.'

She had a point there, Denise inwardly admitted. 'All right. I'll watch out for him.'

'And keep your door locked.'

'Locked.' But locks didn't seem to work always. 'I promise to lock.'

Miss Jessamon prepared to depart, having decided this flat was not 'collectable'. 'Of course he could be a private detective. They do a lot of watching, I believe. Only I don't know whom he'd be watching here. It's usually divorce, isn't it?'

'I'm a widow,' said Denise coldly.

So you say, dear, so you say, thought Flo as she scuttled down the stairs. You have virtually the same sticks of furniture that Mr Burges had and he had the same as the chap before him. It was that sort of flat.

'The murderer is not after me,' said Denise coldly to Miss Jessamon's back. 'Nor you for that matter.' Miss Jessamon was gone, though. 'This murder was a murder of passion, can't you see that, and you and I are not objects of passion.' Since she had lost her husband she had felt bereft of passion.

She went back into the room. In spite of her brave words, she was disturbed. It was frightening to feel watched, even if the figure might be (but might not be) only a fantasy of Miss Jessamon. And fantasies might summon up the real thing. If you thought about a thing enough it sometimes happened. She'd known it.

Denise went to the window to look out. She could see

through the trees to the pavement below. No one there. No one in the street at all. Not on foot. The usual number of cars parked along the kerb, of course, in any one of which an observer might be sitting.

She felt like crying. Even a dry cry, more of a blink than a downpour, usually all she could manage, might be a relief, but she could not summon up any activity in the eyes. The murder of Vivien had upset her much more than she liked to admit. She wasn't herself at all.

'I haven't been my usual self for far too long,' she said, studying her face in the mirror and giving a shake of the head. 'You won't do much good in the beauty business, my girl, with a face as long as a week.'

She adjusted her curls, put on fresh lipstick, and ran a soft, slightly moistened tissue over her face. The shiny look was in fashion at the moment and Elysium liked its ladies to keep in vogue. It suited her anyway and she wished she'd thought of it years ago. She looked and felt younger this way.

She needed some food and she had the usual sort of small errands to do that a woman does whether living alone or not. She collected her keys, one way and another there were quite a bunch, and left the house to walk down the road to where her car was parked.

On the way she took the opportunity to look in all the cars that lined the kerb. All were empty.

It was late-night shopping at the big supermarket so the car park there was crowded, but she found a place to tuck the car. Pushing her trolley down the aisles, steering expertly round other shoppers, she considered what she needed to buy. More than you might expect, as always in her case. She was not a devoted shopper but she was a thorough one.

As she filled her trolley with all the needs of the week, she wondered what the other shoppers would say if they knew she had looked down on a murdered woman. Fortunately, it was not branded on her forehead in red letters; she was anonymous.

She carried her two bags of shopping to the car, where she locked them away. She felt the need to go to the public lavatory across the road from the car park, so she left the car, passing two women discussing married life in critical tones and another shouting at her child. Denise, in her loneliness, thought they did not know when they were lucky.

When she came back, they were still there, but now the child was doing the shouting and a man had joined the two other women. He was silently loading the goods from a heaped trolley into the car. Husband, son or brother, he was not spoken to, the conversation continued over his head. Denise got in her car and drove away.

Miss Jessamon had heard her go, closing the front door which had a distinctive sound to it. She grew uneasy when Denise did not return as soon as might have been expected from someone just going shopping, or paying for the papers, or taking a walk. Miss Jessamon, although good at guessing, did not demand of herself that she got everything right. Might be a good idea, she thought, as she settled in front of the television, to get in touch with the police about that man seen watching the house. She herself might have made a good detective, she sometimes imagined; she had listened to a very interesting talk in Merrywick one evening by a woman detective called Daniels and said to herself: that job would suit me.

But later in the evening she thought she heard the sound of the door closing. And Denise was certainly there in the morning. So that was all right.

Chapter Six

At this time Superintendent Father, who was the head of the CID unit based at Prince Consort Road in Windsor, housed in a new and custom-built unit, was deeply occupied with a large-scale fraud case which engaged most of his attention. It was a secret investigation, code-named BLIND ALLEY, which had drawn off a clutch of his best officers. There was complete silence on BLIND ALLEY, no one was supposed to know about it, although speculation was rife.

In addition, his new Inspector, moved in from another district, Fred Elman, a man looking to climb the ladder quickly, was dealing with a very nasty multiple killing in Slough which, because of its racist overtones, was getting all the media attention. His team also needed experienced and seasoned officers to deal with this critical investigation, which demanded more than the usual patient, foot-plodding interviews, and banging on doors not readily opened, while ignoring snubs, anger and hints of violence.

So Dolly Barstow had been given charge of the third case, the murder of Vivien Charles, which was attracting only local attention and not getting television or radio coverage. For which Father and Elman were both heartily thankful.

But however they were rated by the media, the method of setting up an investigation was the same for each case and each team.

There was always the Major Incident Room, known as Miriam. In the investigation into the death of Vivien Charles, this room was in an old church hall round the corner from Dulcet Road. People came to the front office where

Receivers took in all information, passing it on to the Office Manager who was a kind of long stop. Or, if the information seemed important, it went straight to the Investigating Officer. Dolly Barstow, in this instance.

Indexers put statements on to computer files, numbered by statement, and cross-linked with the person who took the statement. Copies were sent to the Statement Reader who underlined all salient points.

An Action Allocator sent out the errands that resulted from all this and which, hopefully, moved the investigation on a stage.

Such a room, in an important case, called for about sixteen officers. Three such investigations were draining the relatively small CID force, so that Dolly's outfit in St Mark's had what was left after the cream had been taken.

This investigation was code-named FANTASY because of certain elements which everyone had noticed. No one was willing to give it the code-name WITCH.

FANTASY was being worked by Dolly Barstow, who was receiving information and initiating action. But the team remained under the nominal charge of Inspector Elman, who in turn looked to Superintendent Father. Neither man knew each other well or had worked together for long, there had been a lot of changes and promotions recently. Old hands had moved up and away, some of whom Dolly had known well, others whom Charmian had co-operated with on an earlier case in Windsor, and new men had come in.

There was a kind of housekeeping that had to be done, which was how you might describe the questioning of neighbours who might have witnessed anyone entering or leaving the house in Dulcet Road, the necessary checks on all those who knew Vivien Charles, such as those in that little circle of so-called witches, and those that she had worked among in her last place of employment. Her bank manager and her doctor all had been visited and questioned. This was a routine process that must be gone through. From it nothing might come, but it was the classic way in which a case was built up.

Technical reports on forensic debris and fingerprinting all had to be collated. It was a big job on a small case.

Dolly was taking action and receiving reports on FANTASY, but so too were Father and Elman. She was receiving specialised comments and analysis from Charmian Daniels. The other two were not. Maybe they saw her reports, maybe they did not read them.

Their ideas and those of Charmian Daniels and Dolly Barstow were not the same.

Thus it came about that the conclusion that Superintendent Father and Inspector Elman arrived at about the nature and identity and motive of the killer were not the same as that of Charmian Daniels.

For a time, it was possible that Dolly Barstow had a third and yet different idea.

Chapter Seven

In the evening of the day after this event in Denise Flaxon's life, not to mention that of Flo Jessamon, and more than a week into the investigation, three women sat round the table in Charmian's kitchen and drank coffee as they often did lately. A kind of companionship had sprung up between these three very different women at three different stages of their career. Charmian, established, successful, but beginning to ask the sort of questions of herself she would not have asked earlier in her life; Dolly Barstow, feeling lucky to be befriended by Charmian, just building up her career and subordinating everything to it; and Kate, artistic, impulsive, full of love, who was interested in everything and questioned everything. Willing to give the answers, too.

There was another factor behind their meetings: the police investigation, of which Dolly was only one outer edge, and Charmian an honorary member, and in which Kate had no place at all but was passionately absorbed, was daily turning out results and they wanted to talk over what came in.

It was not the best of times in their lives for any of them, none of the three was very happy, which was perhaps yet another reason that they hung together. There is a companionship in mild depression. A state of mind all three shared at the moment. Charmian because of her hand and with what that disability seemed to imply about her own nature; Dolly because she seemed to have lost interest in sex and at her age that was worrying; and Kate because she was beginning to doubt if life intended her to be an architect after all, and a wandering scholar she would not be.

The only happy creature in the room was Muff the cat, who had come bounding in through the window, after what she considered a very satisfactory outcome to her territorial duties (a little blood, skin and fur had been lost on both sides but nothing to count) and was delighted to find an audience of three women, one of whom, Dolly, she sensed did not like cats but was looking trainable. Animals can always teach other animals, and some animals are better than other animals. It is only a question of establishing your ascendency. Muff landed firmly on Dolly's lap, claws hooking delicately into her skirt, a nice bit of tweed.

Dolly patted Muff's head with a careful hand, reluctant to admit to Charmian that she feared cats. 'Good puss,' she said.

Kate was in the kitchen making the coffee and heating the milk, on health grounds she refused to allow them cream. Muff, having made her point with Dolly, leapt away to wind herself around Kate's ankles, suggesting softly that cats also benefited from a drink of warm milk as evening came on. In her case, no coffee please, it spoilt a good saucerful.

Kate had, of course, been listening to their discussion on the death of Vivien Charles in Dulcet Road as she laid out biscuits on a plate and brewed the coffee, adding her comments as they occurred to her.

'Funny all that flitting in and out.' Kate spoke from the cooker where she was watching the milk in the pan. 'Door open so Mrs Flaxon can get in, then someone in the house when you go back. Makes you think, doesn't it?' She looked at the saucepan. 'I love the way milk froths up and goes all kind of solid just before it boils over.'

'Don't let it boil over,' said Charmian in alarm. 'I hate cleaning that cooker.'

'I had noticed. And you might have noticed, Godmother, that your efficient godchild had given it a good clean and polish. It is now as new.' She poured the hot milk into a jug which she put on the table in front of them, placing beside it a plate of shortbread.

'What did you make of Mrs Flaxon?' said Charmian.

Dolly considered. 'Nice woman. Very nervous. Shocked, I suppose. Not that I blame her. Not pretty what she walked into.'

'Good witness?'

'Oh yes. Clear and succinct.'

'What did she make of the fact the door was unlocked and she could walk in? Any idea? Had it happened before?'

'No, on a previous visit she had rung the bell and been let in. This time she let herself in after ringing the bell and getting no answer.'

'She could see the door was unlocked?'

'She said she tried it. One does, you know, in that situation; I've done it myself.'

'Did you get any good from the forensic traces? Or perhaps there weren't any worth speaking of?'

'There were a few, more than I expected really. A bit of dark cloth stuck to the sink. A sort of tweed apparently.'

'Useful if one ever finds a likely suspect.' But not otherwise, Charmian thought. Still, to be preserved and treasured just in case.

'Scraps of skin on the door. Probably from the killer who may have been wounded. But it could have come from the victim herself. And there was a hint of something interesting about the blood. Two lots apparently. But the lab people say that everything needs a lot more work, and they were only giving me guesswork because I pushed.'

She paused, and then said, 'I think the blood is going to give us a lead. Perhaps even a shock. Or anyway say something striking. I just get that impression.'

'More to come from Dr Leatheram then? Is Leatheram dealing with blood and tissues these days?' She knew Leatheram from an earlier case, a tough but subtle man.

Dolly nodded. 'Tom Leatheram, yes, he's good and doing his best, but you know how it is, forensic evidence can give you proof when you have someone lined up, but only hints of where to look otherwise, if that.'

'But worth having.'

'Oh, sure.'

'Fingerprints?'

'Oh, in plenty. Mostly of Vivien, but a few unidentified. Again no use until we have a set of fingers to match them with.'

'Did the neighbours see anything?'

'Mostly out at work all day. You know what it's like in an area such as Merrywick, most of the couples are young and have jobs. Two careers, two cars. The next-door neighbour, who was home with a cold, says she saw Mrs Flaxon arriving. She knew her because she had seen her before. Can't say what time, a vague lady, but Flaxon gives us the time herself.'

'Time of death?'

'They won't be pinned down to a few hours. But about six hours before she was found. That makes it morning. Possibly early morning.'

'Or late morning.'

'Or late morning,' agreed Dolly amiably.

'Well, we won't talk about alibis then.'

Dolly laughed. 'As you would expect, none of the ladies in that little group would admit to having anything so undignified as an alibi. In the mornings they stay at home doing the housework or cooking. Caprice was in her shop, but she makes no claim she was there all the time or could prove it. No witnesses, no alibis.'

But they both knew that this was how it usually went in an investigation.

The orthodox police view at this time, largely unexpressed, but an assumption by such as Inspector Fred Elman and Superintendent Father, that they expected to be able to prove, was that it was a 'group crime'. By the women. They were guessing but they were basing it on past experience and a guess was as good a place as any for a beginning.

Dolly's picture was the same in many ways: she blamed the coven, and feared to name the killer. A man, not the women, that was how she saw it.

But the scene that was forming in Charmian Daniels's mind was more complicated. She thought that the others might be looking in the wrong place. Her gaze would be turned in a different direction. She also thought a man was guilty, but was prepared to be found wrong. In many ways she was the most experienced and sophisticated person who was dealing with this murder, and it was her suspicion that the motive for this killing might not be sophisticated at all.

All saw the pregnancy as important.

Charmian drank her coffee and crumbled a slice of shortbread. 'This is good stuff,' she said with surprise. 'Homemade. Did you make it, Kate?'

'Annie. She's on a cooking kick. Is it a good sign or a bad sign, I ask myself?'

Dolly looked puzzled. 'Must be a good sign surely?' She had never met Kate's mother.

'You don't know Annie. It might mean that she has quarrelled bitterly, passionately, for ever, with Jack. Although I must say it's usually curry or chutney or ginger cake when she does that. Something hot.' Kate's eyes glittered. 'And when she's really mad, then she puts in lots of onions and garlic in the hot stew and it is very purging. Annie says it is healthful.'

'I never thought of cooking as an expression of anger,' said Dolly.

'Oh, it's done all the time.'

Charmian thought of all the toast she had burnt and the casseroles she had overcooked in her brief married life and accepted that there might be something in it.

'Shortbread seems pretty mild,' she observed. 'Especially when sprinkled with sugar.'

'Yes, it has to be a good sign.'

'Why don't you just ask your father how things are?' Dolly could quite see one might not ask Annie. She did not know Annie Cooper, well-known artist and potter, but she could see that one would treat the creator of dangerous curries with circumspection.

'Oh, Jack never knows. He never knows when something is going to hit him. Always a surprise to him.'

76

But not to his daughter, Dolly thought. Did children always know best?

'And what did you make of Mr Fox?' she asked Charmian.

'Good-looking. Interesting.'

'Yes, he is certainly both of those things.'

'Vulpine.'

'That too,' said Dolly.

Kate said wistfully, 'I wish I'd met him. I'm in the mood for a foxy man. I think I might join the Merrywick witches.'

'Don't do that.' Charmian was sharp.

'Why not?'

'Because you ought to keep out of things you don't understand, and especially out of things I am professionally engaged in.'

'Wow,' said Kate. There must be something powerful about these witches to make her godmother so forceful.

Dolly stirred her coffee. 'Mightn't it be a good idea if she . . . well, joined up? We might learn more about the group.'

'Infiltrate, you mean?' said Kate joyfully.

'It's obvious I shall get nothing more, they know who I am now,' went on Dolly. 'It's not professional . . . But it might work.'

'I love the idea,' said Kate. 'Perhaps you could sign me up. Special Policewoman Kate Cooper.'

Charmian shrugged. 'Kate will do what she wants, as she always does. But officially, No.'

'Oh, it was only a joke. Don't be stuffy. But if they've lost their virgin figure, as you hinted Vivien might have been, only, of course, she wasn't, then they might be quite keen to get me.'

'You'd better keep quiet about some of your own activities then,' said Charmian drily.

'But what is it you think they are up to? Corrupting the young? Sacrificing to the Devil? Since I might be a sacrificial object I'd like to have some idea.'

Charmian remained silent so Kate looked at Dolly Barstow.

'I have no idea,' said Dolly. 'But since a murder has come out of it, I should like to know myself. I think there is something rotten going on in that circle somewhere.'

'Do you think they killed Vivien as a sacrifice? Or because she turned out not to be a virgin? If they knew. Oh, I can't believe that of Birdie Peacock, she's such a lady.'

'Ladies can kill.' Charmian put down her coffee cup with a bang. A little liquid splashed on the table, Kate got up for a cloth to wipe it clean.

'If there's enough emotion and passion around.' Kate cleaned the table and refilled Charmian's cup. 'But they don't seem that sort.'

Too old, was what she was really saying, but naturally would not say so in front of her godmother and Dolly, both her seniors. Dolly knew what she meant, though, and gave her a wry look, before throwing in her own comment.

'They seem very ordinary. And very matter of fact about what they do. Caprice dyes her hair, Birdie Peacock goes to Keep Fit classes, and Vivien, who was about the most insignificant of them all, was learning German. Witches with hobbies. It's not what you expect.'

'You can't expect them to go round on broomsticks and wearing dark pointed hats,' said Kate. 'In Merrywick that would get them noticed.'

'I think they like publicity. Within reason.'

'You look thoughtful, Godmother.'

'I want to find out what turned a group of harmless, well-intentioned women into a lethal band,' said Charmian. 'If that is what happened. That is going to be my function in this case.' Dolly would have the procedural stuff in hand, and would keep her informed. 'Which of them is the most important, in your opinion, Dolly?'

'At first I thought Birdie Peacock. Now I think it is Caprice.'

'You don't like Caprice, do you?'

Dolly shook her head. 'I don't trust her.'

78

'I'm going to talk to Miss Peacock and to Caprice. That's a start.'

'And then?'

'Oh, that's obvious, isn't it, and I shall want your help there: find out more about Vivien Charles. She may have been the youngest and the most insignificant, but she was the one who was killed. She had a life outside Merrywick and that's what we need to find out about.'

'Do you think her pregnancy matters?'

'Oh, it matters all right,' said Charmian absently.

While Kate was washing the coffee cups, Dolly said, 'I had a strange telephone call today. Well, perhaps not so strange, we get a lot of odd calls, you know that. I suppose I mean interesting. It was from a woman, middle-aged and educated from her voice. A Miss Jessamon from Slough. She asked to speak to someone dealing with the Dulcet Road murder in Merrywick. Said a man had been seen watching the house where she lived. All small apartments. She said she was frightened it might be the murderer studying a new victim.'

'Not likely, is it? Is that all? She gave no reason?'

Dolly shrugged. 'No, which made it one of the nonsense calls we do get about a major case . . . But when I checked the address I saw it's where Mrs Flaxon lives, and that did interest me.'

'I suppose Mrs Flaxon may have told her she found the body.' Two women under one roof, talking together. Wasn't it likely that Mrs Flaxon had sought relief and comfort by confiding in a neighbour?

Dolly said, 'I got the distinct impression that the woman had no idea that Mrs Flaxon was connected with the case.'

Kate could be heard talking to the cat, making soothing noises. Presently she carried Muff in. Muff lolled peacefully in her arms, enjoying the petting.

'This poor creature has a torn ear. She's been in a fight.'

'I'm afraid it's Miss Eagle's cat. He will push through the garden fence and Muff resents the intrusion on her territory.'

'What's he like?'

'Lean, black and muscular. Too much for Muff.'

'I expect she gave as good as she got,' said Kate, indignantly. She and Muff had a special relationship. 'I'll have a look next time I see him.'

'You don't think we have seen him?' said Dolly. 'In Dulcet Road?'

Benedict was a witch's cat and might go anywhere and return from anywhere, but one thing Charmian was sure of was he was too wily to get caught. If that had been Ben leaving Dulcet Road on one dark night nothing would ever be proved.

Charmian did not answer directly. One black cat looked so much like another.

'I have to admit I rather like the cat. But I think he's a devil.'

Dolly went back to what was really on her mind: 'Do you think Mrs Flaxon is in any danger?'

'It is possible. She may have witnessed more than she realises. Let me see her statement again, will you?'

Dolly nodded. 'Will do.'

'What description of the watcher did Miss Jessamon give?'

'Ah, well, there you have a point. She didn't see him herself. Another flat-dweller did. Said he was a very ordinary-looking chap.'

Charmian thought it over. Was it worth pursuing? Yes, it was.

'I'll talk to Miss Jessamon and the other tenant. Then I'll interview Mrs Flaxon. See what I can get out of her.'

Soon after this, Dolly left and Kate picked up her coat and announced her intention of visiting her mother.

'I might stay the night. We've got some family business to talk over.' Both Annie and Kate were the beneficiaries of a large family trust and one of the things the Coopers, mother and daughter, were always level-headed about was money. 'So don't worry if I'm not back.'

Kate patted Muff on the head and departed.

It was a warm, light evening, with a full moon, a witches'

moon, Charmian thought. Or did witches prefer the dark? She stood at her garden door while Muff flitted past her, a striped shadow disappearing into dappled shades of trees and bushes.

No good calling her back, it was one of those nights when Muff was not going to hear.

Without putting on a coat, Charmian walked round the corner towards Miss Eagle's house in Abigail Place.

It was not all dark as might have been expected, but one of the rooms on the ground floor was lit up with curtains undrawn. Standing out on the road, Charmian could see into the house.

A sitting room. But remarkably bare and plain with all the chairs drawn back to the wall. Almost an empty room. The room of someone who needed space. Air all around them. It was possible that there had been a meeting there. A session of witches. Or possibly a standing of witches?

Because there, standing in the middle of the room, absolutely naked, was Miss Winifred Eagle.

Someone who needed air and space all around her body.

She looked muscular and spare, obviously having no trouble with her hands, a good deal healthier than Charmian felt herself at the moment.

As Charmian watched the light went out. Not as if Winifred Eagle felt she had been observed, or cared either, but more as if that part of the evening was over.

Charmian crept back home, although why she should feel the need to be unnoticed when Winifred Eagle so obviously did not, she was not sure.

When Charmian got back to her own front door she noticed a small object lying on the step. It might have been there before she left by the back door, or it might have been put there while she studied the surprisingly nubile Miss Eagle.

A little, roughly shaped human figure, fashioned out of plasticine, endowed with marked female characteristics and a needle through both eyes.

It had been given a rough, carrot-coloured mop of false

81

hair made of cotton, so Charmian took it to be a represen-
tation of herself.

She stood looking at it without touching it. A feeling
of some excitement came over her.

She had asked questions, she had prodded, she had
probed, and she had got this in return.

We're rolling, she said with satisfaction.

As she stood there, Muff leapt from the bushes, seized
the object with a cry of joy and disappeared the way she
had come.

Chapter Eight

As was her wont with any specially valued capture, Muff had laid out the little figure, carefully, tenderly, in the middle of the pillow on Charmian's bed.

She had sped in through the opened bedroom window while Charmian took her bath, laid out her trophy, then, having done all that honour and natural instincts demanded, she had curled herself up in tranquil sleep at the foot of the bed.

'Thanks, Muff.' Charmian emerged, rubbing her hair dry. 'And this time I mean it. I wanted to see that object. This is evidence, pet, not a billet-doux.' She stood looking down at it. 'Yes, it's me all right. Meant to be, anyway.'

She popped the unpleasing simulacrum of herself into a plastic envelope, which she then sealed. It was unlikely that much information about its creator could be got from it after its trip in Muff's mouth, but Forensics could try. And you never could tell.

'But it means I got under the skin of someone. Badly. And since it is so personal it is likely to be someone I actually spoke to. That means the Merrywick Witches, and Mr Fox.'

The envelope went into a drawer of her bedside table. A book to read lay open: some poetry tonight. Milton, no less. He made her feel educated; also there was something very soothing about his rolling verse. A few hundred lines of 'Paradise Lost' and she would be asleep.

A soft breeze was blowing through her bedroom window, ruffling the curtains. She stood there looking out for a few moments, enjoying the soft night air.

She could just see the top of the castle itself where the Royal Standard fluttered. Beyond lay the Great Park with its avenues and leafy walks, mile upon mile, the old hunting grounds of the mediaeval kings of England: Norman, Angevin, Plantagenet and Tudor. The castle itself, originally planted there in his usual firm fashion by William the Conqueror to intimidate and hold down the neighbouring countryside, had long been a small township in itself. Within the castle walls live several communities, at its head the court when the sovereign chooses to visit, and then the more permanent inhabitants like the Poor Knights of Windsor and the clergy of the Chapel of St George. Not to mention the military, whom one might expect in a royal castle and of whom the Governor is the Great Officer. The Hanoverians were fond of the castle (George III more or less lived there), Queen Victoria was the Widow of Windsor, while the present Queen is said to regard it as her home.

The castle is a strong image, rising up boldly with the town at its feet, and one which Charmian delighted in. It seemed to record the march of the centuries in stone: Norman keep, Plantagenet chapel, Tudor library and Victorian dairies down by the road to Old Windsor. Bewildering to the visitor, Old Windsor, the original old English village, is some miles along the road, nearer to where the Anglo Saxons forded the River Thames at Staines.

The town itself, daily crowded with visitors, has a few eighteenth-century houses near the castle but is largely a Victorian creation. Charmian's own small house in Maid of Honour Row was over a hundred years old but unpretentious. Probably a small tradesman and his family had lived in it when it was built. Or a castle servant walking up the hill to his work each day.

Charmian did not run through this catalogue as she looked out of her window while Muff snored gently on her bed, but it was there at the back of her mind. She certainly remembered the visitors because only that day she had had to leap backwards into a bush of thorns to avoid being mowed down by a coach full of Japanese tourists, swinging down the wide curve of the High Street towards the River. She had a pair of laddered tights in the rubbish bin to prove it. To add to her fury, the constable on duty had said to her with a wink: 'Trying to commit suicide, Miss?' She resented the wink more than the remark.

But now she was simply enjoying the night air; there was an avenue of limes not far away whose scent joined with her roses. A British Airways jet from Heathrow sailed overhead, but the noise did not worry her, she hardly noticed it. It was a comforting sound, it was home.

When there had been no houses, no roads, no traffic, nothing between the castle and the old forest, there had probably been ghosts and witches.

Hern the Hunter was said to appear in the Great Park, although the sceptical Charmian knew she would never see him. George III was reputed to hang about the castle itself and take the salute from the Guard on occasion, but she did not feel she was likely to see His Majesty either, he only appeared to soldiers. If there had to be any ghosts she thought she would have preferred to meet Sir John Falstaff, that patron of Windsor ales – one stood as good a chance of meeting a literary ghost who had never existed as a real, dead man.

As to witches, the records testified to the prosecution of a couple of witches living in squalor amidst a clearing in the Great Park. But that was in the late seventeenth century. They had come up for trial in the assizes but the case had been dismissed, the Age of Reason having dawned and the alert and pragmatic Lord Justice Meadowcraft being on the Bench. He who had said that if witchcraft could cure his gout, then he would believe in witches, but since it could not, then he did not.

Probably Meg Cottar and Joan Longcross had been no more than midwives and healers, perhaps a bit too zealous for their own good. Or just unlucky. Mothers die in child-birth and babies are stillborn even now, and litigation sometimes comes of it, but gallows do not loom, only compensation.

White witches, that was what Winifred Eagle and Birdie Peacock claimed for their sisters of Merrywick. Perhaps something in the air round here summoned up the idea of witches.

'Only I think I am on the side of Lord Justice Meadowcraft.' She flexed the fingers of her right hand. If the Witches of Merrywick could cure her hand, then she would believe in them. No sign of it so far.

But, as Kate would no doubt point out, you have to ask.

'Can't see myself asking,' said Charmian out of the window. 'That sort of thing ought to be a free gift.'

She wondered what Winifred Eagle had been up to, dancing naked in her room.

Had Winifred Eagle delivered the missive on her front doorstep, sometime between Kate departing and Charmian finding it?

And had she done so stark naked? For some reason the thought amused Charmian.

'I wonder if she met Kate going down the road?' Charmian wondered as she drifted off to sleep. 'If so, Kate is the only one of us who would remember to say good evening.'

There was no sign of Kate next morning so presumably she had spent the night with her mother in the flat in Wellington Yard (where Charmian had once lived). Unless, Kate being Kate, she had taken off for Tibet or Beijing, from which city she would eventually send a postcard, signalling her arrival.

Before dressing, she took another look at the image in the plastic bag. It looked less like her this morning but was still an unpleasant object with the orange locks, which had clearly not been well stuck on, beginning to come apart from the scalp.

Charmian, having taken an anxious check of her weight on the bathroom scales, decided that grapefruit and black coffee were her fate that morning. It must be all the shortbread and rich cake that Annie had donated to the household, most of which she herself had eaten.

She put on a neat suit as being appropriate to a day of interviews and applied a low-key make-up. As she brushed her hair, she noticed a lot seemed to be coming away with the brush. Tiresome. Perhaps the new hairspray did not suit her. She must consult her hairdresser, an old friend and enemy called Beryl Andrea Barker – Baby to her friends – who had a beauty shop off Peascod Street.

After a moment of hesitation, and feeling ashamed of herself, she went to the little doll and stuck its hair back on as firmly as she could. Better be safe than sorry.

When she went out to start her day, she saw Miss Eagle working away in her garden. She was wearing a clean print dress with a tiny belt round the waist; she looked a different person from the naked lady of the night before. It was hard to believe it was the same woman.

There was something about that respectable, genteel figure that riled Charmian. I'll give you a miss today, my lady, she decided, let you get on with it. Whatever it was.

Winifred Eagle raised her head as Charmian approached. 'Good morning.' Her pale eyes were at once sharply focused yet without expression, like a blackbird looking for a meal.

I've never liked birds, thought Charmian. Whatever you say about the pretty creatures, when you get close they don't have a pleasant look about them. Eagle, Peacock, too many birds altogether. Had they fluttered towards each other because of their names? 'Nice morning. You've started work early.'

'I like to get ahead with the garden before it warms up. It's going to be a hot day.'

Charmian responded mildly, not saying much. Winifred went on brightly: 'And I like the open air. It's so nice to feel the air about one.'

I bet, thought Charmian. About you and on you. She felt her head itch and passed a hand over her hair. Drat it, this was self-suggestion. Mercifully no hair came away in her hand. But Miss Eagle noticed.

'Are you all right, Chief Superintendent? Have you got a headache?'

Charmian shook her head, trusting no hair fell out. 'No,' she said shortly.

Miss Eagle gave a hopeful stare, waiting for more from Charmian, who said nothing, but gave a polite smile and walked off.

Out of the corner of her eye, observing Winifred, she thought she looked disappointed, as if a communication of some sort would have counted for something. Might have been expected?

Was it possible that Winifred meant Charmian to have seen her naked form last night?

I was right not to talk to you, Winifred Eagle. Whatever you and I might be, we are not friends.

Charmian drove what she called the country way to Slough. It took longer but on a fine summer's day was something to enjoy. Of course, it was hardly country really, but there were trees and grass and stretches of what had once been farms. There were horses in the fields, and you did see the occasional cow, although whether they gave milk or were just there for decoration, Charmian had never made up her mind.

She was soon in heavy traffic, but she knew the back roads to Woodstock Close where Denise Flaxon lived, with the shop Twickers around the corner. She had followed the route taken by Denise on the day she had made her statement in Merrywick Police Station, but it was the way taken by everyone who desired a quiet ride.

Charmian sat for a while in her car, observing the whole street. Cars lined the kerb, some of the vehicles looked as though they were never moved, but stayed there week in and week out. The gutters were littered with bits of paper, empty drink cans and other trash. It was a familiar urban street scene. Windsor was clean, wealthy Merrywick positively sparkled; this street was grubby. But nevertheless, the houses that lined it were solid and not unprosperous. Number twenty, where Denise Flaxon lived, even had window boxes full of geraniums on the ground-floor sills.

The front door sported three bells with names underneath. Flaxon, on the top, Jessamon underneath, Schmidt beneath that – so to the Schmidts must go the credit for the window boxes.

Charmian was about to press Miss Jessamon's bell when she was forestalled. The door was opened by a small, stout woman, dressed in a red and white cotton dress with a kind of bandana of matching material round her head. The dress was tightly belted, producing the illusion of a waist where no waist rightly was.

'No need to ring the bell. I saw you from the window and recognised you. I'm Flo Jessamon. Come in, come in.'

Charmian found herself in a dark hall, smelling of dust and dried flowers. It was carpeted in red with an old oak table on which was a brass gong, and a scatter of letters which looked as though they had been posted years ago and got no welcome when they arrived.

'How did you know me?'

'You gave a talk in Merrywick a summer ago. I was at it. Enjoyed every word.'

'Thank you.'

'That was a terrible business there that year, wasn't it?' Flo Jessamon was referring to a series of brutal killings in Merrywick in which Charmian had been involved.

'Very.'

'And have you come about the man I reported?' Flo was pleased. 'Didn't think we'd get anyone as high-up as you.'

Charmian consulted her notes. 'You reported the matter, but the man was actually seen by a Mr Schmidt.' Miss Jessamon started to speak, but Charmian, recognising a compulsive communicator, went on: 'And is Mr Schmidt at home?'

She had become aware of a smell of frying onions and something strongly savoury like paprika seeping through the cracks of the door at the end of the hall.

'Yes, I believe so,' said Miss Jessamon reluctantly. 'But . . .'

The door to the Schmidts' flat opened and a tall, thin lady appeared holding a milk bottle.

'Oh Flo, I thought it was the milkman. I wanted to complain. This milk is off.'

'But, he's such a nice man. It's your refrigerator, Louise, I've told you that before.'

Behind Mrs Schmidt appeared a small, mouselike figure who had to be Mr Schmidt.

Charmian went forward, managing to circumvent both his wife and Flo Jessamon who were now engaged in a mild argument on the matter of refrigerators and nice milkmen.

'Mr Schmidt?'

'Dr Schmidt.'

His wife turned her head with a look of surprise, but she said nothing. Miss Jessamon did.

'Oh, Ferdy, you aren't a doctor, are you?'

Charmian ignored all this, although it did introduce a certain doubt in her mind as to the value of Ferdy Schmidt as a witness.

'My wife is very concerned about the quality of the milk,' he said softly. 'It makes her quite violent. Are you the Health Inspector?'

There is no doubt, Charmian thought, that I carry an aura of authority with me. I am an Inspector of some sort, anyway.

But Ferdy Schmidt answered lucidly enough when she got her question through to him.

'You ask about the man I saw watching the house? Yes, he was standing under the tree watching. One notices a thing like that when one has lived my life. Such a life. It should not be inflicted on a dog.'

But he described the man. Tall, not young, not old either. On the whole he thought he was probably in his late thirties. Wearing jeans like they all do. Casual. He sounded disapproving.

Tall? But anyone would seem tall to the small Mr or Dr Schmidt. About the clothes? Yes, on this matter, Charmian felt she could rely on Ferdy Schmidt. He looked a careful dresser himself, although dressing-gowned at that moment.

'Stayed there quite a time. Then he went back to his car and sat there. Still watching. He thought I couldn't see him. But I could.'

'Oh, he had a car. Can you describe it?'

Ferdy nodded. 'A red Cortina. Nothing special.'

'I don't suppose you noticed the number.'

'Wait.' Ferdy held up a hand, he disappeared into his own apartment from which the smell grew ever stronger. He reappeared holding a piece of paper, which he handed over to Charmian. 'Here. You take it. I thought there was something funny about him, so I wrote it down.'

At this moment the milkman appeared, and the attention of Mr Schmidt was demanded by his wife.

Flo Jessamon gripped Charmian's arm, the delinquent arm whose hand refused to write, and said, 'You should listen to me. I saw the man too.'

'I thought you didn't.'

'He came back, he came again,' said Flo in triumph, 'and I was watching from my window.'

'That was lucky.'

No luck about it: she had been watching on purpose, staying on guard all day.

'So can you give me a description?'

Flo obliged. 'Not *very* tall. Medium height. Fair hair going grey. I was looking down so I could see he was going bald on top. Just a bit. Clothes? Oh, they were lovely. Beautiful dark suit. Very expensive, I should think. Yes, I might know his face if I saw it again, but I was looking down from my window, so I could not see his features so clearly,' she added regretfully.

'Did he have a car?'

Yes, he had had a car and he had parked where she could see it.

'No, I couldn't say what sort of car. I don't know enough about them. But it sort of matched his clothes. Expensive. The colour? Oh, dark blue, a very dark blue. Smart.'

91

Unlike Mr Schmidt she had not taken a note of the number but she remembered it began with a G.

A this-year registration number. If Flo Jessamon was right then the smart dark blue car was new this year.

But the red Cortina observed by Mr Schmidt was at least four years old.

The description of the men clashed as well.

Two different cars? Two different men?

She saw Miss Jessamon looking at her for approval. 'Thank you, that's a real help,' she said gently. 'It may have nothing to do with the murder, but it's interesting.' For reasons you know nothing about. 'I see you have a Mrs Flaxon living on the top floor, do you think she saw anything? Is she in?'

Miss Jessamon looked doubtful. 'She might be. She comes and goes. You could try. I thought I heard someone go up the stairs.' One couldn't watch all exits and entrances, and no one regretted that more than she did. Especially with this rumour she had picked up (in the Post Office, she always did well there for news) that it was Denise Flaxon who had found the body of that poor girl. Flo had not told the Schmidts this little nugget, and wasn't going to. Keep it to herself, her property.

Charmian rang the bell for the top-floor apartment. Getting no answer – bells did not always work – she mounted the stairs and knocked on the door.

There was no answer. She tried again, but, getting no response, turned away.

There was someone sitting in the corner of the room, well away from the window. But that person was not Mrs Flaxon and did not wish her well.

Charmian drove past the shop Twickers on purpose. It was open with a customer just coming out, so she found somewhere to park the car and walked back.

Caprice was behind the counter on which was a great earthenware bowl filled with what looked like a mixture of dried herbs and flowers. She was busy transferring this to little cotton bags, and then tying them up with red ribbon.

'For insomniacs,' she said. 'Put one of these on your pillow or round your neck and you will sleep well and have good dreams.'

'I'll buy one.' And Charmian laid some coins on the counter.

Caprice looked surprised. 'Have it on me.'

'Do they work?'

'I've never tried. I always sleep well, and as for dreams, I tell myself what I want to dream and then I do it.'

Charmian crushed the little bag in her hand. It gave a sharp nose-pricking smell, not entirely pleasant, but strong. It might contain some sleep-bringing drug, although she wondered if the dreams that came with it would be good.

Caprice watched her with a slight smile. 'Risk it,' she said. 'See what you get. It's not the same for everyone.'

'Isn't it?'

'So I'm told.'

'What's in it?'

Caprice gave the bowl a stir. 'Oh, I don't know. Odds and ends. This and that. Birdie mixes it up.'

'I'd like to meet her again.'

'Easily done. She's always in and out. She'll be in later today.'

'I'll be back.' If not today, then some other time. Charmian was interested in Twickers and all that went with it.

Seen in bright sunlight, the shop was more like an old-fashioned apothecary's shop with a touch of a food store.

'Did you ever think that Vivien was being watched?'

'No, I never did.'

That seemed short and sweet.

'But if she was, it would be a man.' Caprice gave a short laugh. 'She was that sort. Harmless but a man's girl. It showed.' She wasn't herself and that showed, too.

Charmian did not ask her about the little figure left at her door. No point. If Caprice knew of it, she was not the sort to confess. But Charmian thought the shop was, somehow, its provenance. It matched.

When she had gone, Birdie Peacock emerged from the back room where she had been hiding.

'So she's gone. What did she want?'

'She wanted to know if Vivien was being followed. Or watched.'

'She was, of course.'

Caprice nodded. 'And she wants to talk to you.'

'Then I'll keep out of the way.'

'She looks to me the sort that will keep coming back.'

Caprice returned to bagging her wares. 'I gave her a bag of this. With my compliments.'

Birdie laughed. 'You are a devil. Well, good luck to her.' Then she looked down at the counter with its scatter of coins dropped by Charmian. 'Oh, look, you didn't give it to her. She paid.'

Caprice followed her gaze. 'Damn, damn and damn.'

She subscribed to the view that between the witch and the victim no money should pass.

Charmian drove back to Maid of Honour Row, where she fed Muff. She thought longingly about eating something rich and filling on her own account, but recognised that her waistline would never stand it, so she settled for a drink of ice-cold water. Then she extracted the small image, whose outline seemed to get more blurred with time and put it in her pocket. Almost all the pretend hair had fallen off by now. Altogether it was an unpleasing object.

She decided to walk to the church hall where the Major Incident Room for the murder investigation was set out. All possible windows had been opened inside but it was still hot and stuffy and people were working in shirt sleeves. A bank of green screens linked up with the main police computer were offering information without comment. A uniformed WPC moved languidly between desks distributing printed sheets. No one seemed full of energy, but those who recognised Charmian at once took on a brisker air.

She saw Dolly in the opposite corner of the room.

'We ought to have air conditioning.' Dolly fanned herself.

'It is humid; I think a storm might be blowing up.'

Dolly found yet another window to open. 'Try getting even a fan out of our lot!'

'Things not going well?'

'No. We're no nearer finding out who killed Vivien. No one saw anything, no one heard anything and no one admits knowing anything. There's just one woman neighbour who says she might have seen a man outside Vivien's house taking a look, but she isn't sure. You can talk to her if you like, but I don't advise it. She suffers total recall about a life without incident. You even get the dripping tap and what the plumber said.'

Charmian thought her young friend needed bracing. 'Oh, come on, you know every case has a patch like this, then things move on.' Mostly but not always. They both knew that as well.

Dolly was not to be done out of her grumble. 'As far as I'm concerned it looks like nothing, nothing and nothing.' But her face lightened. 'There, I feel better now I've said that. And there is this,' she threw a sheet of information towards Charmian. 'About the blood in the kitchen.'

Samples of blood had been taken from Vivien. In the ABO blood grouping system, Vivien had group B which is shared by just over eight per cent of the country's population. Vivien's blood group could also be broken down into yet another grouping system of an even rarer sort.

Charmian looked up. 'So far so good.'

'Read on.'

There were traces of another person's blood by the sink and on the handle of the knife used on Vivien. This could have been the murderer's blood. When analysed this was found to be group A – a more common group shared by about forty per cent of the population.

'So, we know the blood group of the killer. What we don't know is his name or address.'

'That isn't all,' said Dolly. 'The outfit that searched for blood traces did a thorough job. Read the last paragraph.'

On the door handle leading to the hall there had been

found further blood traces: this turned out to be an unusual AB group.

'You see the scientist doing the analysis is careful to point out that this is a very provisional analysis,' said Dolly. 'But it could show the presence of a third person.'

'Two men, two killers?'

'We don't know the sex,' said Dolly.

Charmian walked to the window to look out. The sky was darkening by the minute, and a few heavy drops of rain were already falling.

'I have evidence of two men being involved.'

Two cars, two men, two murderers?

'Check this car number for me. It may not be entirely accurate but see what you get. Might be a red Cortina.

'Right.' Dolly studied the number. 'I'll let you know.'

'Do that. And I've got something else for you,' Charmian said, putting the image in the plastic bag down on the table. 'It was left on my doorstep. Presumably to ill-wish me. See what Forensics can get out of it.'

Dolly examined it distastefully. 'Nasty. But why to you and not me?'

'I suppose someone dislikes me more.'

Or she could just be a neighbour who had only to pop round the corner. But she did not say this aloud. No prejudging.

'And there's this.' She dropped the little bag on the table. 'Get this analysed, will you? Picked it up at Twickers. Said to aid sleep. I'd just like to know what sort of sleep you get.'

'Do what I can. The lab will start to hide when they see me coming with all the work I'm bringing in.'

'Do them good,' said Charmian heartlessly. Between her and the technical services there had long been a war.

'Don't you want to try it yourself?'

Charmian put her hand in her pocket again. 'Got another. I paid for the first one and helped myself to a second.'

Dolly, who had picked up a bit of this and that at her meetings with the group, looked thoughtful. 'Was that wise?' she asked. On the whole she liked to pay for what she got from places like Twickers.

Kate and Muff were both in the house in Maid of Honour Row when she got back. Kate was rubbing Muff down with a towel.

'This poor cat has been shut out in the rain and got wet.'

'All her own fault,' said Charmian absently. 'She would go out.'

'Oh, you are hard.' Kate herself looked as though she had got wet, her long fair hair was trailing over her shoulders and her jeans were damp round the ankles.

'Glad to see you back. Quite a storm, wasn't it? Dry yourself, why don't you?'

'Always feed and groom your animals before you do yourself.' Kate nodded her head towards the kitchen table on which stood a ginger cake and a jar of pickles.

Charmian read the signs with a prickle of apprehension. 'How's your mother?'

'Fine. Sends her love.'

'And Jack?'

'He wasn't there,' said his daughter. 'I'm not sure if Jack's in or out at the moment. Mum cooked a lovely fish chowder followed by lemon mousse. That goes either way.' She pursed her lips. The lemon had been sharp and sour. But served with cream. Annie was often ambivalent. 'She's sent us a jar of pickled onions.' That was definitely a downward sign.

'I haven't been idle, I went into Twickers and sounded innocent,' went on Kate, releasing Muff. 'I have got myself invited to the next meeting of the Merrywick Coven. I said I'd seen their notice in the Merrywick Library. Said I had the best intentions, of course. Nothing wicked. I've joined up with what you might call the white witch side. You know, good thoughts, and being kind to animals, especially cats. But I suspect there is a black side and I am looking out for it. Let you know.'

But when Charmian showed her the bag from Twickers,

97

she picked it up with the kitchen scissors and threw it down the waste pipe, setting the steel jaws to work at chewing it to bits. Then she flushed the bits away.

'I just wanted to try it,' protested Charmian.

'The thought is not worthy of you, Godmother, and I am not going to let you. I don't like Caprice and I don't trust her. She'd damage you if she could.'

Like sending nasty little images through the door. 'Why?'

'Because of what you are. Who you are. Have you ever crossed her or a friend of hers?'

Charmian was thoughtful. 'I might have done.'

'And there's something else. I hung about Caprice's shop and heard what I wasn't meant to hear. They've turned on Josh Fox. It's a hunt.'

Chapter Nine

By the next day the storm had passed, but the heavy rain had depressed the roses which hung heads down, heavily. Fallen petals lay on the grass, leaving little brown stubs of calyx behind.

Charmian drank her coffee in the kitchen, looking out of the window at the ruins of her garden. But it would pick up, give it a day of sun and you would never know there had been a storm.

She wished she had such resilience.

Her hand was moving well, willing to wash, eat and pick up a lipstick. But it still seemed reluctant to do any written work. She had managed to hide this disability as far as possible from Dolly Barstow and Kate, but she saw them watching, and somewhat resented their tact. In many ways she felt she would have preferred it if they had grumbled.

Perhaps she wanted reproof, punishment. There was a thought, and not the first time it had come to her. But she refused to accept it as truth: she had killed in self-defence. A man had tried to rape her, then to kill her, she had killed him. She didn't exactly feel guilty, but a little depressed perhaps. And when she met someone like Josh Fox, then she wanted to run away. Frightened.

She poured some more coffee and added a spoonful of honey.

'I ought to learn to laugh at myself,' she said, staring out of the window. 'I'm just not good at it.'

Kate could do it, although not often; Dolly used to be good at it but had lost the trick lately, which might be due to meeting the witches, because witches cannot laugh;

while she, Charmian, as now she realised, had taken herself seriously all her life.

She poured a saucer of milk for Muff (and who takes themselves more seriously than an adult cat? – no jokes there), then went to get dressed.

A work-day so she dressed appropriately in a dark blue linen dress with a matching jacket. It showed her mood.

Where Charmian had to go next was entirely up to her. She was on leave, her office was not in touch, although her secretary sent on those letters she thought Charmian would wish to see or ought to see (she was a girl who took a stern view of life) and added to it a summary of important events in the last few days, so that Charmian knew exactly what was going on behind the scenes of an important fraud case now being prepared for prosecution. (A celebrated female academic was involved which was going to be a shock for everyone.) She knew also that it looked a strong possibility that the six men found buried in a mass grave had been put there, possibly when not dead either, on the orders of a woman. True that woman had been a Celtic queen, dead herself these two thousand years, but both cases showed what women were capable of when given the right motivation.

Both these affairs interested her, but she wasn't going back to them. Those two cases had been largely solved, the death of Vivien Charles had not.

She wanted to know the answer, she wanted to be able to look down at a collection of evidence, a pile of notes and say: So that's how it was. Somewhere in this puzzle would be the Witches of Merrywick, she hoped that they were right in there and as guilty as hell, because she was beginning to dislike them but they might merely be innocents caught up in it all.

On the other hand, she had a strong feeling that two men were involved in the murder of Vivien Charles. Nameless men, so far.

Those two men had to be found and identified. The car number ought to help there. The police machine, of course, was better at this sort of task than one solitary searcher, so she could leave that to Dolly Barstow. Or could she?

100

She thought that Dolly did not seem quite so keen on the search for the men as she was. Dolly would rather go straight after Caprice. No prejudice, of course, Dolly just felt Caprice was a likely candidate. But which, all the same, suggested to Charmian a name for one of the men.

Why not hypothesise that one of the men was the enigmatic and attractive Mr Fox? Josh Fox. If she felt anything strongly about him, and, as it happened, she felt several things very warmly, it was that this was not his name. He was a contrived person, not exactly made up, but kind of pasted together.

He might be a writer, she could accept that as part of his persona, because that might be the reason he had interested himself in the Witches of Merrywick. Writing them up. Was this what had angered the coven and turned them against him? She was on to something there, she thought.

But one of the other feelings she had (apart from questions about his identity) was that she had somewhere met him before. And not as a literary figure.

The third strong impulse she had about this man was that he was as attractive as Dolly had said. She couldn't quite explain this since he was not remarkably good-looking if considered dispassionately. She had read that warlocks exuded a special smell from their skin to attract witches. Perhaps this was the case here. She must consider it. If so, he had it under control and was well able to manipulate his own attractions.

All in all, someone to keep away from, except professionally, and she hoped she would be able to do it.

From Dolly she had a dossier on all the people concerned: names, ages and addresses with telephone numbers. Thus she had Josh Fox's address. He had provided an address in Slough: Elm Street.

Charmian consulted a map of the district which showed her that Elm Street was close to the city centre. Digging around in her memory she decided that it was a newly developed street close to the big covered shopping complex.

She telephoned Dolly Barstow who answered the telephone with a groan. 'So early?'

'It's not that early.' Charmian looked at the clock, it was nearer nine than eight o'clock.

'Depends when you got to bed. I was called out in the night. Caprice's shop had a break-in, and they got me out to look at it.'

'Why you?' Why hadn't the uniformed outfit handled it?

'I think because Caprice screamed for me so loudly . . . And there were certain strange features about it.'

'Such as?'

'Door hadn't been forced. Almost like an inside job.'

'And was it?'

'If so, I can't imagine why. But the lock was nothing much, anyone who could put his hands on a big bunch of keys could probably have found one to fit. And the burglar alarm was set off, Caprice has a sophisticated system, but an insider would have known about that and watched it.'

'Might not.'

'Well, we'll see. Fingerprints and so on may help.'

'Anything missing?'

'Caprice claims she doesn't know yet. Says she has to check. I'm not a hundred per cent sure she's telling the truth.' Dolly really disliked Caprice and would get her for something if she could.

'Do you think she's got any drugs there? That perhaps she's marketing them under the guise of natural medicine?'

'Not the hard stuff,' said Dolly cautiously. 'I think I'd know if she was on that list, even if we hadn't got proof, I'd probably know her name. But the lighter stuff, yes, it has occurred to me, but no evidence. Of course, we will be having a look round for any traces.' Caprice probably guessed that the search for fingerprints was not entirely disinterested. 'Someone may think she has, of course, and hence the search of the shop. It was really turned over.'

'Kate informs me that the coven has turned on Josh Fox. Any connection with the attack on Twickers?'

Dolly was at once interested. 'So they've quarrelled? Wonder why? There might be a connection, but I don't see it. My feeling is that it's personal to Caprice.'

Charmian considered. She didn't like Caprice any more than Dolly did, but in every group there is a scapegoat and it might be that Dolly had elected Caprice as this without the woman being guilty of anything but not being likeable. 'What about the blood?' she said. 'Are you getting all contacts tested?'

'Yes, they've all agreed to be tested. I've made appointments for them all with a lab technician.'

'And do they know why?'

'No, but I expect they can guess. I'll be there if I can. I hope they go in one after the other and I'd like to watch their faces as they look at each other.'

'You're really vindictive.'

'I am,' said Dolly with feeling.

'One more thing . . . about the break-in at Twickers, in which the door was not forced. Does it remind you of anything?'

'It does indeed. Dulcet Road. Someone got in there without a key.'

'I wonder if Caprice got the shop through Blood and Sons of Merrywick?'

'The same thought occurred to me. I'm getting it checked, but so far I haven't got the answer. No one felt like getting Mr Dix up in the small hours.' Then she said crossly, 'Do you know you've woken me up and I don't feel a bit like going back to sleep.'

'Just a minute.' Charmian ruffled the pages of the dossier supplied by Dolly Barstow and the investigating team. 'I see I've got Josh Fox's address.'

'Of course. He gave it, and it's there.'

'Anyone been to check?'

'Someone did. Not me.' There was a strange note in Dolly's voice.

'And he does live where he said?'

'Let's say he's got a place. As for living, who knows what he does or where?'

'What are you getting at?'

'The address is up a staircase above a jewellers in Slough.

103

There is a brass plate on the door with the name J. Fox on it. And that's about all. The jeweller is a tenant, does not own the property and does not own or claim to know Mr Fox. Why not go yourself and take a look? Elm Street, got it?'

'Exactly what I intend to do.'

She had a list of addresses of which Elm Street was only one. Abigail Place, Garter Road, where Birdie Peacock lived and strutted, a number of addresses belonging to various women who had come to meetings of the White Witches and paid a subscription even though they were reluctant now to be named as sisters or members of the coven. She had Caprice's home address and the address of the office in Hatton Woods which had last employed Vivien Charles. Twickers, she thought, she could give a miss.

Charmian made a fresh pot of coffee because she could hear Kate moving around, and assembled her thoughts.

A woman had been killed in her own house, stabbed to death with a knife from her own kitchen.

That was where you had to start. Then around her had been placed symbols of witchcraft. But of black witchery, the sort of symbols that were famous or infamous in the annals. Anyone could have looked them up in a book and then put them together. Thus laying suspicion on the witches.

Or someone who had hated the victim so much that even after doing the killing there was the additional need to degrade. Some killers were like that.

The dead woman had been a member of a coven of professed witches, but witches, so they claimed, of the harmless, well-intentioned sort. Healers, feminists, worshippers of a female deity, not a black thought among them. Herbalists, not alchemists. Life worshippers not Satanists.

Such worthy women, but had a change come over them, turning them into something not quite so harmless? They had produced a victim. The motive for whose killing was not yet known, but had surely to do with her pregnancy. And that brought in a man.

And two men were alleged to be watching the house in which lived the woman who had discovered Vivien Charles.

Kate said over her shoulder, 'What are you thinking about?'

'Men and women,' said Charmian absently.

Kate laughed and took some coffee in a mug. 'That's a start, Godmother.'

'And do they commit different sorts of crimes?'

Kate shrugged. 'I don't think so.'

'Neither do I. But when they commit murder does a man set about it in a different sort of way to a woman?'

'I suppose this all has some practical application to Vivien Charles?'

'Of course. The killer leaves his or her imprint on the crime. All that we do leaves traces of what we are.'

'So what do you see?'

'I see a killer who hated the victim, who probably hated the witches. Or at least wanted to implicate them. I see a very angry face but it may not look angry. A face with a mask on it.'

'Why do you say that?'

'Because I think Vivien trusted her killer. Possibly let the murderer into the house. Certainly let the killer come close. There was no struggle.'

The profile of the victim was important, too. She had to get nearer to Vivien, this young woman who had been pregnant, whose child had shown signs of malformation, which could have been one consequence of a shock when some weeks into the pregnancy. She was a girl whose life might have had many a shock in it.

'I love to hear you talk,' said Kate admiringly. 'You make it sound so simple. But I know it's not. You're looking for someone whose face you can't see. Do you think you'll know where to look?'

'Beginning to think so,' said Charmian. 'But it needs some straightforward police work.'

'And what's that?'

'Looking and questioning. Plodding, you know. It's one of the things police do. Boring stuff but necessary.'

105

A long time since she had done her own leg work, but she was enjoying the prospect.

Kate let Muff out of the window, then went to the front door to collect the post. She sorted out those that were addressed to Charmian. 'Here you are . . . Did I hear the telephone?'

'Yes, I was talking to Dolly Barstow. I woke her up. She had a late night. Twickers was broken into last night.'

'Do you think it's anything to do with the murder?'

'It could be coincidence. They do happen. It's just possible the person who broke in may have been hopeful of finding drugs. Dolly is inclined to think so. It may have nothing to do with the murder at all. But I think it has.'

Then she said, 'I'm off out.'

'Classic police work as laid down by Chief Superintendent Charmian Daniels? Where to?'

'I have an address.'

In fact, she had several.

Josh Fox had an address, another address, a brother and a sister but no wife, he had a mother still extant, he even had another name. He could be set in a context.

But, as yet, not for Charmian or Dolly Barstow. For them he was floating free, they needed to anchor him.

The police computers, of course, are full of details about all sorts of citizens of the United Kingdom. You get your name on one just for living at the wrong address (once raided for drugs, never mind if you did not live there then) or for buying a car that had been stolen, and of course you did not know, but Mr Fox was adept at keeping himself out of computer files.

Confident in himself and in his anonymity, he was surprised when he felt the blow on the side of his head. His attacker had a hand on his shoulder and was wrenching him round. Stronger than he'd suspected.

'Look here—' he started to say.

He debated fighting back, but that was not good business,

was never good business. A blow on his cheek got him before he could do anything about it.

He staggered back.

Elm Street was a very new and still raw shopping precinct. Charmian thought she would be surprised if anyone knew anything about anyone. No long-standing friendships among shopkeepers here.

A big chain store was flanked on one side by a dress shop advertising a sale. From the look of the window the sale had been running for some time and was probably quietly heralding the closure of the shop for dresses and its reopening as something else. There was a shoe shop with, next door to it, a small jewellers. Between the shoe shop and the jewellery shop was a white door with a small brass plate on it. The plate was dull and unpolished.

J. FOX

Nothing else. There was a bell on the side of the door and a knocker. Charmian tried both but got no response.

She wasn't sure if she had expected one. On the whole she thought not.

The jeweller surveyed her over a glass case of golden ornaments, studying her with caution. She looked harmless, even respectable, but these days you had to be sure. And she didn't appear to be buying.

No, he had not seen Mr Fox, would not really know Mr Fox by sight if they met in the street.

Yes, Mr Fox did have visitors, or he believed so, they rang the bell and were admitted. More than that he did not know. He heard a telephone ring there.

No, he had no idea if Mr Fox was there now.

Charmian went back and rang the bell again. No one came. She stood looking, and frowned.

She thought she detected a small smear of blood on the white paint by the door handle.

Chapter Ten

By the early afternoon, Dolly Barstow was anxious to talk to Charmian. She telephoned the house but got no answer at first. Finally Kate answered the call. No, she had no idea where her godmother was, nor did she know when to expect her back.

'I'm going out myself. Hairdresser. I'm trying that friend of Charmian's.' Kate tossed her long mane of expensively cut hair. The Italians, she thought, were best for long hair, but she would try this woman that Charmian thought so good.

'Andrea Barker?' Dolly knew all about Beryl Andrea Barker and her criminous career, having gone to some trouble to find out, but she was not among those allowed to call her Baby. Miss Barker had taken part in at least two episodes of Charmian's professional life, she was both friend and informer. 'She's good.'

Her own hair needed attention, she ran a hand over it. She was near enough to Kate's age to share her own strong feelings about hair, but otherwise the two young women were unalike. Dolly had settled cheerfully into a career with a firm structure up which you crawled or jumped: she meant to jump. Kate was a wanderer, a perpetual student, a pilgrim always looking for the next holy shrine to worship at. Dolly lived in a neat, quiet flat which she owned. Kate chose to be homeless, perching with whomever would give her space. They were almost two different species, as if *homo sapiens* was trying out variations to see which would last better in time and space.

The other side of the coin was that the two women liked

108

each other and cared about Charmian Daniels who had befriended them both. They did not discuss her behind her back, her presence was strong enough, even in her absence, to put a stop to that, but now Dolly spoke.

'How is she?'

Neither of them would mention the hand trouble, although both knew.

'What happened to her was bad, and the trouble is she won't admit how bad,' said Kate soberly. She had known violence and death in her own life, been capable of it as well, she knew what violence could do to you. 'It's screwed her up.'

'Do you think so? She's enjoying the chase at the moment.'

'I wish it wasn't a witch hunt. It brings in all sorts of things she'd be better without. It's why I am giving a hand.'

It was amazing, Dolly thought, how often the word 'hand' crept into the conversation.

'You know what I think,' went on Kate, 'it's a pity Humphrey is abroad and the sooner he gets back the better. Straight sex is the answer.'

'Kate, you! I don't think you are a feminist at heart. You are an old-fashioned married woman.'

Kate laughed. 'Any message for Charmian? Anything I can tell her?' she probed hopefully.

'I mustn't be too explicit, but I've spoken to Mr Dix of Blood and Sons.'

'The estate agents in Merrywick?'

'Yes, just tell her that, and also that something else has turned up at Twickers. I can't say more. Say I'll telephone again.'

And Dolly tried later, got the answering machine but left no message. She had more to say than a machine could manage. She wanted both advice from Charmian and to share with her something that might, or might not, be a joke.

She was telephoning from the hall in Alexandria Road.

★

109

In the CID Incident Room for the investigation into the murder of Vivien Charles it sometimes seemed as if Vivien was the least important person in this puzzle. She had become an enigma built into a murder mystery, but who had already, willy nilly, contributed her blood and certain physical specimens now in bags and frozen.

Birdie Peacock, Winifred Eagle and Caprice Dash occupied a line of chairs in the hall. They sat in a row and hated each other. They were getting on each other's nerves. As well as this specialised, personalised, name-taped hate, there was a more general hate for everything and everyone in the room. They had been given the privacy of a screen but the noises of telephones ringing, voices muttering away in reply and the bustle of people coming and going was clearly audible to them.

They hated each other because they were being blood-tested and they hated the whole set-up in Alexandria Road because it was where they were being tested. If the ill-will of witches could work the whole room would have gone up in smoke. Possibly the whole town. If witches' blood had any power then the young woman who was drawing it up in a syringe would have been reeling away in horror instead of speaking to each in turn with a calm smile as she swabbed each arm. That was how strongly the women felt.

'Don't worry,' she said to each arm, never looking at a face, 'you won't feel anything, and I don't need much blood.'

A small quantity was taken off into a tube, neatly labelled, signed and dated. Somehow to each witch lady it seemed insult added to injury that they should have to admit to having owned what was taken from them.

'May it curdle,' thought Winifred Eagle. 'May it destroy all it comes in contact with, may it turn into a million milling, writhing worms as she works with it.' That would give this confident, white-coated figure the creeps. But it wouldn't happen. It was occurring to this professed white witch that you couldn't turn your colours and become black just as it suited you. Her curses had no power.

110

Caprice said nothing as she presented her arm, and tried to feel nothing. She would be very surprised if her blood helped any investigation. Not if she could stop it.

Birdie Peacock told the technician that she was a blood donor and could supply the name of her blood group, but the information was not demanded of her. They must do their own analysis she was told.

The young woman was bland and uncaring, she really preferred her donors dead.

'Just wait a minute, ladies,' she said. She reported back to Dolly Barstow, who was working at a desk in the corner. 'Do you want them? They are in a rotten mood. I don't think they appreciated coming here.'

Dolly shook her head. 'They can go. You've got two more bloods to take?'

'That's right. After which I'll get back to the lab. You want the results quickly, I suppose?' She was used to Dolly Barstow.

'Even quicker,' said Dolly with a smile.

She turned over the report she had in her hand of the break-in at Twickers. She wrinkled her nose. Not nice. But many things were not in police work. Nor in laboratory work, for that matter.

'You've got that other specimen?'

'I have.' The technician was cool.

'Will it give you the blood group of the donor?'

'With luck.'

Dolly was apologetic. 'Not a nice job for you.'

'You get used to it.'

All the chairs were empty now and in a few minutes Josh Fox arrived to fill one. He had a great bruise down one side of his face which had drawn blood.

Dolly observed him with interest. That's a nasty wound. He wouldn't have shown himself around with that if he'd had any choice. All the same, he's being very obliging, he's come here. I wonder what that means, if anything.

Josh Fox was dealt with quickly and soon departed, pretending not to see Dolly Barstow.

111

'He looks as though a visit to a first-aid clinic wouldn't do him any harm,' Dolly thought, but she felt pretty sure he was not going to go.

This case was like a sardine tin: when you opened it up, you were surprised how much it held inside.

She reached out a hand to the telephone to try to reach Charmian once again, then she drew it back. Better wait now till she had something on the blood groups.

Last of all, by appointment, Mrs Flaxon came in to have her blood tested. Just in case, they had said. But Denise was not worried, she knew no blood of hers had been shed in that house in Dulcet Road.

'I'm not a bleeder,' she told herself. 'Not a weeper, either. Any blood I had to shed was shed when I lost my husband. Vivien Charles wouldn't get any blood out of me, no one could.'

However, the technician did extract a few drops, she was good at her job. 'Your veins are very hard to get at,' she said, when her task was accomplished. 'Thank goodness, they're not all like you.'

Charmian Daniels drove away from Elm Street, leaving Slough and its shopping centre behind her to find the area in Hatton Woods where Vivien had worked. She had to fill out her picture of the victim. Vivien Charles had had a life before she came to live in Merrywick, a strange move in itself.

Know the victim, Charmian told herself, and you are that much closer to knowing the killer.

This was not true, of course, of a random, 'by chance' killing, when the murderer might not even have met the victim before the violent moment of murder. But all the indications were that the murder of Vivien was deliberate and planned.

Hatton Woods was a busy district well on the way to Central London with several large office blocks lining the main road. It looked clean, prosperous and anonymous. The offices had enormous car parks, there was a tube station not far away and a sign post indicating the way to the railway station, romantically and misleadingly called Hatton Woods. There wasn't a tree in sight. But it was impossible not to hear the drum of heavy traffic on the two motorways that looped round the area. No one lived in Hatton Woods, you came here to work then got away as soon as you could.

Accordingly there were very few shops but several fast food bars where you could grab a sandwich or a hamburger roll together with a carton of coffee and eat while you talked. Or even while you walked, Charmian saw at least two people munching long thin rolls full of something that smelt savoury as they walked through the streets.

Charmian sought an empty spot to leave her car, in a side road by the railway station which was otherwise dedicated to a frozen food depot. She saw a traffic warden pacing the street, a large lady who seemed to be eyeing Charmian hopefully. But she had found a parking meter into which she had fed the necessary coins so she was able to smile back. She could have pulled rank, explained she was a police officer on duty, but she wanted to be anonymous. The woman had not recognised her. Good. 'You know you've only got two hours, dear? It's restricted parking.'

Charmian nodded. 'I've noticed.'

'Just saying. Lot of pressure on parking round here.'

Perhaps something official in Charmian's manner came through because the traffic warden gave a quick nod as she turned away. Charmian did the same, so they marched smartly in opposite directions.

It must look like a dance, thought Charmian, as she walked away. Come on now, laugh at yourself, this is a chance. Two human animals, strange to each other, meet, declare their territory then take a neutral stance, and part.

She found the office building in which Vivien had worked. It was one of the smaller places on Furnival Street which itself was a passageway between two arteries: Kingsway North and Kingsway South.

Cay-Cay PLC, the firm which had employed Vivien, appeared to occupy all three floors of the building. A

113

fine brass plate (beautifully polished and no blood on it) displayed their name outside the big glass doors, behind which stood a uniformed doorman. A small fountain played in the marble hall beyond. Whatever Cay-Cay did in the business world it looked well placed. It either had money or could borrow it.

On the other side of Furnival Street was a wine bar which promised glasses of Bordeaux and Chablis. Charmian crossed over the road, noting that although a very new area the roadway had been artistically cobbled to look old. The wine bar, called Nathanial's, was painted dark green both inside and out, deliberately cave-like. Deep red tiles made a cool, hard floor. The Bordeaux was served in thick white glasses whereas the Chablis came in a thin green glass.

The place was about half full, with several people standing along the bar and a few couples eating at the tables which lined the walls. There was a pleasant cool smell of wine.

Charmian ordered Chablis, and asked for a telephone.

The barman nodded towards the back. 'You'll find one there in the corner.' From his detached manner, she decided he was not Nathanial, if indeed that gentleman existed at all. 'It's quiet enough there.'

She dialled her own number so that she could listen to her answering machine retailing her messages. A routine one from her office, and one from someone trying to sell her double glazing for her windows. A call from her mother reminding her that it was her sister's birthday next week. (She forgets mine, why do I have to remember hers? Charmian reacted, but then Jess had always been the one her mother protected, while Charmian had been the 'bright' one who could look after herself.) And Dolly's brief messages.

Charmian drank her wine, ate a sandwich and refused the conversation of another Chablis drinker on the next stool, who was bored and looking for some interesting company. Any other day and she might have taken him up on the offer but today she was working.

Early afternoon inside the Cay-Cay building was a time of quiet. Unnatural quiet. The air conditioning kept the

114

temperature cool, the darkened glass on the windows created an air of false tranquillity. Charmian felt it to be false because people hastened through the halls with tense faces and lowered but anxious voices.

She herself was inspected by the Chief Personnel Officer, a tall, blonde woman wearing dark glasses and a sincere smile, both of which seemed to be part of her professional equipment. A small red notice on her desk said she was Bridget O'Neill. Two police officers had already visited her, asking questions about Vivien Charles, but her training prevented her showing surprise or, for that matter, any emotion at all at seeing yet another one. But no doubt, over the years in her job, she had learnt blankness was for the best.

'I had very little contact with Vivien myself.' She consulted a file in front of her. 'In fact, she left very shortly after I arrived here. Vivien worked in Presentations. She was PA to the Deputy Head, Roger Armitage.'

'Can I see Mr Armitage?'

'I'm afraid you can't, no. He's no longer with us, he works in the States now.' Since this was clearly not going to satisfy Charmian, she offered: 'You can see the other girls in Presentations.'

She showed Charmian to the lift. 'Was it anything special you wanted to know about?'

Who she went to bed with, that's all. 'Just feeling my way,' Charmian said blandly.

Bridget pressed the appropriate button. Charmian wondered how Miss O'Neill got about in those spectacles in this dark world. Perhaps they had tiny little holes in them through which she really looked. Her smile never shifted. 'Presentations, third floor, room A.'

What did they present in Presentations in Cay-Cay? Charmian wondered as she sped upwards in a dusky lift.

There was more light on the third floor as was no doubt necessary for those preparing Presentations, although of what, except that it appeared to involve time and money, Charmian had no better idea when she left than when she

115

had arrived. Somehow, in the carefully modulated atmosphere of Cay-Cay, such direct and brutal questions like What do you do? and How does it make money? seemed too coarse. Clients were probably too subdued to do more than sign and accept what was on offer.

But she steeled herself to be direct to the girls with whom Vivien had worked, amidst a bank of winking amber screens, and found that in their rest-room, where the light was brighter and the fittings less expensive, it came easy.

There were two of them, one dark-haired and plump, and the other taller and thinner with carefully tangled fair curls. They were both married and showed no surprise at her questions.

'She didn't have anyone here,' said the dark one. 'Roger was a dish but he had his sights set higher. Knew his own value, did our Roger. Anyway, I don't think she fancied him. You can always tell. Don't you think, Freddy?'

'Oh, you can,' said Freddy. She was taking the opportunity to touch up her eyeshadow. 'Those bloody screens flickering all the time ruin your looks. Don't know why, but they do.'

'Don't touch me,' said the other one. 'I'm fine.'

'Oh, you're indestructible, you.'

'About Vivien,' Charmian reminded them.

'Oh, she had someone,' said Freddy. 'We all do. Naturally. It might have been several someones, but it wasn't here. We'd have known, wouldn't we, Shelagh?'

'Couldn't hide it, it's a village. But Viv kept things quiet. Didn't talk about herself much.'

What a nuisance, Charmian thought, a murder victim who was the soul of discretion was no help to anyone.

'Do you think she talked to her family?'

They both laughed. 'Would you?'

But they passed on freely what they did know about Vivien which was a lot: they knew where she had her hair done; where she liked to shop for her clothes (Wardrobe and Next with occasional forays to a shop they called Harvey Nich's when she was in funds); that she was size twelve most

116

of the time but could drop to a ten; that she put on weight quickly but soon lost it, and that her favourite colour was blue.

Charmian sensed that Shelagh knew more about Vivien's sex life than she had admitted. This was confirmed when the girl offered to show her out. As they got to the door, Shelagh said, 'She did have someone, you know. I was sure of it when she left. She didn't flash an engagement ring or talk about her wedding dress but there was someone. She wasn't going to another job or she'd have told us. No need to keep that quiet.'

'And there was need to be quiet about what she was doing or where she was going?'

'She was secretive about it. Mum as the grave. We wondered at the time. I asked her outright, but she just laughed and didn't answer. Perhaps he did come from round here even if not from Cay-Cay. But whoever he was he may not have given her a ring, but he gave her a beautiful bracelet. I saw it. Nothing cheap about it at all.'

'No idea who the man was?'

'I suppose it was a man, I don't think she was a lezzie. Not sure of it. But who he was, or where she could have met him . . .' Shelagh shrugged. 'No, I can't help you there.'

'Did you like her?'

Shelagh hesitated. 'Not my sort of girl.'

'What does that mean?'

'Into things I couldn't take. Not exactly superstitious but odd. I like things down to earth. Viv said her grandmother was a witch, could charm warts away, that sort of thing. For that matter, my grandmother could, but I didn't call her a witch, just a lucky old lady. She won fifty thousand on the pools and she didn't drop dead. She married her butcher because she liked his red hair.

Charmian digested all this information. It fitted in with the picture she was beginning to form of Vivien Charles: a physically attractive, but emotionally immature girl. Not very bright, perhaps, but interested in ideas.

She looked speculatively at the lively and informative

117

Mrs Shelagh Duncan. 'You've answered questions already, I know. But did you pass on all this?' DC Darty had been assigned to ask the questions at Cay-Cay House, so her records had informed her, and got precious little out of it as far as she could see. Maybe he hadn't written it all down.

'No, I didn't. He didn't get much out of me.' Shelagh gave a satisfied nod. 'He called me "Love". Only once, but it slipped out. That shows what he thought of women. I like a man to be a man, but I'm not going to be patronised.'

Charmian went out into the street thinking that she must pass the word along to Dolly Barstow to tell the young detective, tactfully or otherwise, to tone down his image.

Across the road was a tall, narrow building seemingly sculpted of dark glass which glittered evilly, and richly (that too had to be said), in the sun. Cay-Cay's side of the road was now in the shade.

A great stone logo spread itself across one side of the bronze double door. No glass doors, no welcoming doorman here; it looked as though you had to shoot your way in.

The logo, which must relate to the name of the business so splendidly housed, seemed to be a large EL. The style reminded her of something. She considered what that could be, then decided that it was the sign she had seen all over Merrywick and Windsor, and most notably in Blood and Sons, Estate Agents, Merrywick.

HOMELINE.

For the first time there was a link, a visual one, however tenuous, between two parts of the life of Vivien Charles.

Not much, but something.

She went into the wine bar to think about it. They really kept a very good Chablis. She ordered another glass and decided to see what she could find out about the EL outfit. What they did, who they were and who worked there.

People who worked in wine bars picked up all the gossip.

★

'There are things I have to tell you,' announced Dolly Barstow when she finally got through to Charmian in person.

'Good things?'

'Depends.'

Dolly was at the end of a long and trying day in which she had had to deal with a child assault case, probably perpetrated by a parent, and with a nasty case of poison in jars of honey in a food market. She was, accordingly, tired and fretful.

Charmian, on the other hand, sounded annoyingly fresh and cool. Lively as well. She'd never heard that the lady drank, but perhaps tonight?

'First the blood groups: this is just a flash first report which I forced out of the technician – none of the women tested have blood groups that match anything found in the Dulcet Road kitchen. All were blood group O. Perhaps it is a requirement of witches,' she ended sourly.

'And Josh Fox?'

'A rare group all his own. But not found in the kitchen. It would also preclude him being the father of Vivien's child. You can test for that too, it seems. But he turned up with a bruise on his face and a tear in the scalp. He could have done with a stitch. Someone has had a go at him.' Dolly sounded sad, as if it grieved her to think that beautiful face had been battered.

'I wondered how he was,' said Charmian. 'So someone had hit him?' She considered the blood on his door, would it be worth a check? But she had already concluded that the traces were probably too slight to give much information. 'So we are no nearer knowing the identity of the third person in the kitchen?'

Dolly said, 'Looks like it. A bit of a blank . . . And about the lease of Twickers, a blank there. Bloods of Merrywick had nothing to do with it. Not one of their properties.'

'Any more non-news?'

'Well, the check on the car number was not very productive. But the computer did come up with a number on a red Cortina that was close to the one you offered. Belongs to a man called Edward Elder, an address in Sunbury.'

'You'll go after him?'

'Yes, someone is checking,' said Dolly with a sigh. 'It all seems no-go. And yet I have a funny feeling old Dix knew something.'

'I have news for you there,' said Charmian, cheerfully remembering the Chablis drunk on her second visit to the wine bar, Nathanial's. 'I had a drink after I'd been to Cay-Cay and got talking to a solicitor from an office down the street; he seemed well-informed and willing to talk, and I picked up this from him. There is a link between a firm called EL in Hatton Woods opposite where Vivien Charles worked at Cay-Cays and Bloods of Merrywick. EL has recently gone into the property and estate agency business. A consequence of the Big Bang and the tremendous growth in property values. Among other things it now owns HOMELINE which in turn owns Bloods.'

'I don't know what to make of that,' said Dolly. 'Perhaps old Dix was lying.'

'Have another go at him. Or get one of your citywise chaps on to it. Likewise Josh Fox, that attack on him means something apart from a black eye. People, go for people,' went on Charmian. 'Check the list of employees at EL, see which of them might have met Vivien – in Nathanial's, the wine bar, for instance – and known about property in Merrywick.' Had a key perhaps to Dulcet Road. 'Cross-checking might identify someone who turns up in both places.'

'Right,' said Dolly. 'I hope all these businesses are computerised and can turn up information quickly.'

'Oh, they will be. So maybe, enter the Third Man.'

That was definitely the Chablis speaking.

'And I have news for you too,' said Dolly, breaking in. She produced her trump card, which she had been saving up. 'It starts with Twickers. The break-in, remember? Well, we discovered that the visitor left a visiting card. Know what I mean?'

'Yes.' Charmian was surprised. 'Shows some emotional involvement doesn't it?'

'Could just be a lousy joke from the criminal. I have known it.'

Faeces, *grumus merdae*, the criminal's *carte de visite*. The criminal's nervousness produces an increased peristaltic movement which leads to an involuntary evacuation of the bowels. This is one view. Other people think that the criminal has to mark his identity on the scene of the crime and this is how he does it. So there were two schools of thought, you could take your choice.

Certainly it demonstrates something, Charmian thought. Love or hate.

'Interesting,' she said.

'I think so. I got the pathologist, the one who did the bloods, to run a test on it.' All body waste products carry identifiable traces. 'It was easier than I thought. It seems he or she had some internal bleeding. Possibly an ulcer. So there was blood. And she thinks it could be of a group, the A type with subdivisions, which when combined with Vivien's type, which was B, could have produced what we thought was the third blood type, that rare AB mix.' She ended on this triumphant note.

'So the murderer and the person who broke in at Twickers could be the same person?'

'Yes.' Hypothetically, anyway. It could just be coincidence, which happened more often in life and police matters than was always admitted.

'Pity your expert witness didn't think of it before, instead of getting us all worked up over someone who might not exist.'

'It's only a suggestion.'

'Seems likely. So exit the second murderer,' said Charmian thoughtfully.

There had been Vivien in the kitchen, and her murderer, who had made two. But the blood groups had suggested a third person present. Now this third person seemed to have disappeared.

There had been one man watching the house where Mrs Flaxon lived, who might be the murderer, then there had been another. Was this second person still there?

'Question the two people in Slough about the men who were seen. It may be possible to clarify that situation.'

Dolly had never quite liked the sound of those two men. Denise Flaxon who had found Vivien's body lived in the house in Slough. That was the only positive fact. The rest might be the product of overactive imaginations.

'We don't know those men, if they exist, have anything to do with the murder at all.'

Charmian accepted this, but ignored the comment. 'Don't forget EL,' she said.

Dolly had one last shot to deliver. 'Oh, by the way, that little bag of herbs you picked up in Twickers, the analysis has come through . . . I don't know if it would have given you a good night's sleep, but if you had managed to absorb any through your skin you might have had some nasty dreams . . . Contains a fair amount of dried Black Henbane and the seeds of Thorn Apple . . . Datura, famous for producing hallucinations. I don't think Caprice likes you.'

'I'm sure she doesn't. It was probably her who dropped the little doll on my doorstep. Made it at home, I should think.'

'No report on that yet, I daresay they don't know what to look for. But yes, Caprice has my vote too. Oh well, I'll get the computers busy on the other stuff.'

Dolly sounded cheerful now.

But the computers turned up no one who seemed to have contact with Vivien Charles. No one whom the police questioned in the glossy glass building who admitted to knowing her.

Nor could Miss Jessamon nor Dr Schmidt be shaken in their evidence. Both had seen different men.

Nor could Josh Fox be located, and the blood traces on his front door proved too dried and weathered to be any use at all.

They had entered into one of those periods when nothing seemed to go on and the investigation stood still.

But Charmian hoped that this was an illusion. She had given the witch's cauldron a stir herself.

A day passed in which Charmian visited her doctor who said her arm was coming on nicely, which she took to be doctor-speak for no change and wait and see. She herself was aware of no change.

That evening, her telephone rang.

'Josh Fox here.'

'Ah.' Her number was unlisted, but he had it. Mr Fox must have methods of his own for finding out facts he needed to know. But she did not comment. 'I've been trying to get hold of you.'

'I'd like to come round and talk to you.'

She looked at the clock. After nine and Muff was asleep on her lap. 'Not tonight.'

'No? Tomorrow then? There's something I want to tell you. You're intelligent. I think you'll understand.'

'What about telling me on the telephone, then?'

He hesitated. 'No, it's a face-to-face thing.' They made an arrangement to meet in the morning. Prudently Charmian asked him to come to the hall in Alexandria Road where there would be witnesses. She would tell Dolly Barstow in the morning.

He had sounded less self-confident than the fellow she remembered meeting.

A hunt, Kate had said. Well, someone had attacked Josh Fox already. It would not end there. Events might yet go at a gallop.

Chapter Eleven

On that next day, which was Tuesday, the inner group of witches, the coven – although Birdie found this name distasteful, preferring central committee – were now in session. They were also in a state of some fury.

The object of their fury was Josh Fox.

Ragingly angry and seeking revenge. Winifred Eagle thought it should be physical (she was in a very physical mood at the moment, so much so that Birdie was somewhat anxious about her balance of mind); Birdie herself suggested taking legal action, and Caprice Dash was out for blood and money both.

Money first, blood afterwards.

'Liar, betrayer, deceiver, dog,' cried Winifred with gusto. 'But oh he had a lovely face.' Not so lovely now, today, she acknowledged, a little bruised.

'What a mercy you got on to him, Caprice,' said Birdie.

'I have my contacts,' said Caprice modestly.

So far they had not actually touched Josh Fox, although they were aware that other hands had, and roughly too. He had been sighted leaving the hall in Alexandria Road.

'I'm not surprised,' said Birdie. 'In his trade you do deal with dangerous customers.'

'You might say that of us, too,' observed Caprice.

'Rubbish.' Birdie thought of all her friends, those she met at conferences and witches' weekends (sponsored by SellaSpell Ltd, in which she was a stockholder), her juvenile groups with trips to Avebury and Stonehenge. They were all respectable people.

Winifred said, in a sibilant whisper, unnervingly some-where between a hiss and a moan, 'I could dance on his bare flesh.'

Birdie gave her an anxious glance. 'Don't let anyone else hear you say that, dear.' To Caprice, she murmured, 'She's going over the top.'

'I heard that,' said Winifred. Her face was flushed, her hair escaping from the soft net of matching nylon that usually enclosed it. Such snoods tore easily, she had to buy one a week.

As she straightened it, she said, 'Are you really called Caprice, I've always wondered?'

'Christened it.'

'Such a name. Now that is dangerous.'

'My sister was christened Fortune. She married a man called Goode.' Caprice laughed. 'Just as well it wasn't Bad.'

'I never know whether to believe you or not,' said Birdie.

'In this instance, I am telling the truth,' said Caprice smoothly, although not in a voice that made Birdie believe her particularly.

'I don't think we should have let that young woman, Kate Cooper, listen in to our anger.' Birdie tidied away a few crumbs which had settled near the tray of coffee and cake which she had served for the three of them. She felt that a milky drink and something sweet to nibble settled the nerves and in her opinion Winifred needed settling. 'It wasn't wise.'

They were meeting in Birdie's bleakly tidy maisonette behind the county library in Merrywick. One of her neigh-bours was the head librarian, they were old friends, had been at school together, which accounted for the good publicity their group always got. Birdie lived in an austere way, the principal furnishing of her living room being a large wall display-board of green cork stuck with notices of meetings around the country which she might or might not attend; also a list of members and their addresses, and notes of future projects, she was usually planning something. A Junior Chapter seemed a good idea, she liked the idea of nourishing young minds.

'Couldn't have stopped her,' said Caprice shortly. 'All ears that one. I must say I do dislike that policewoman Daniels. Gets up my nose.'

'You've done your best to get up hers,' retorted Birdie. 'I think the object on her doorstep was a mistake. In lamentable taste, not what we are for, Caprice. I thought better of you.'

'I shouldn't have told you, I thought you'd see the joke.' But it was no joke, when Caprice showed malice, she meant it. 'Winnie dropped it down for me.'

'And look at her now,' said Birdie sharply.

Winifred was not paying much attention, that natural worshipper, who worshipped at more than one shrine before more than one god, was listening to a current deep inside her which was telling her that very soon now she might downgrade the Earth Mother and bow down before Buddha – she saw lovely things in that pale, calm face which attracted her.

'I wonder about Tibet.' Her voice was dreamy. 'We need fresh souls. Old souls.'

'We need the young ones,' said Birdie, her mind on a disciple group at the local comprehensive. The head was very open-minded and having a large percentage of immigrant pupils from all continents was obliged to be liberal about religion.

'So you say. But look at Vivien, she was a young soul, raw even, and what has that brought to us?'

'Josh Fox,' said Caprice, 'amongst other things.'

'He was watching her, you think?'

'Sure of it.'

'Kill him, I say,' said Winifred, forgetting the pursuit of the gentle Buddha.

'That's not respectable talk, we don't kill people,' Birdie reproved her.

Winifred considered. 'I believe I've got unrespectable feelings inside me.'

'Do you think he was the one who broke into Twickers?' Birdie pursued her enquiries.

'I don't know. I don't think so.' Caprice did not know

about the visiting card or the bloody testimony it had held, but she had a gut feeling that the break-in was not Josh Fox's doing. 'I don't see why he'd need to.' Now it had been the police, looking for drugs on spec and covering up for themselves afterwards . . . She could accept that as a possibility, but hoped it wasn't. Probably be in for questioning now if that was the case. No one had mentioned drugs to her, although she hadn't liked the look in that Barstow woman's eyes. 'Bastard,' she said thoughtfully.

'Ah, he was the primitive male principle among us,' said Winifred. 'We needed that.'

'You've got sex on the brain. Do you know his address, Birdie?'

'Of course.' Birdie looked at her notice board. List three, names and addresses, typed. It was the Elm Street address. Charmian could have told her that it was of doubtful value as a resting place for Josh Fox.

'We'd better get him.'

'Let's telephone first.'

Birdie did so and got his answer phone which told her in a pleasant voice that Mr Fox was not able to answer her call at the moment but if she would leave a message he would respond as soon as possible.

Birdie did not leave a message. 'About what I expected. He could be there, though.' She looked with a question at Caprice, her dangerous lieutenant.

Caprice nodded, she knew her part. 'Let's go.'

Winifred gave a little moan of pleasure.

'Any more nonsense from you and we shan't take you,' said Birdie. 'This is business, this man is a menace to us. Has damaged us probably already.'

'And been damaged himself.'

'We don't know who did that. Any more than we know who broke into Twickers.'

'I don't see *really* how he has damaged us,' said Winifred.

'He will pour dirt on us, if we give him the chance. He must have been collecting information. Watching Vivien, and watching us. And for what purpose? That's what we don't know and must find out. Good job that Caprice found out from her friend what Josh Fox really was. And don't say we haven't done anything wrong, everything can be twisted. Besides, it's not just that . . . ' Birdie paused. 'He invaded us. Used us, acted a false part. He deserves to be punished.'

Winifred, while enjoying the idea, still protested. 'Well, I don't know. He never said he was the Devil or Anti-Christ, although I often used to hope he might be.' In her wilder moments, which were coming frequently these last weeks.

'Let's get ready,' said Birdie.

This involved a certain amount of preparation. If they were going to get physical with Mr Fox, even if he was not a representative of the Devil, precautions had to be taken. Some practical, some more spiritual.

A change of clothes, into something older, was only sensible before an encounter which might be bruising. Birdie put on a printed cotton dress, several seasons old and easily washed. Winifred was given a shirt and a pair of trousers, Caprice borrowed an old raincoat to cover herself. Birdie quietly added a bit of plastic to protect vital parts. Plastic, being man-made, was neutral, whereas newsprint could be downright dangerous.

The clothes themselves came from a pile freshly laundered, while the raincoat was straight from the dry cleaners. Birdie had a selection of such clothes, she took them to the nearest Oxfam shop if no other use came for them. The bundle from which she selected today's garments had been intended for Afghan refugees, although what comfort they could have made of several Laura Ashley dresses and a waterproof from Biba (for Birdie had once had her fashionable period) was not clear.

In fact, she was obsessively clean, washing herself and her clothes, firmly and daily. As Winifred said, 'You're always sure of seeing a clean pair of knickers drying in Birdie's bathroom.'

She herself, as Charmian had noticed, favoured the cleansing and liberating effects of nudity. It was not, however,

128

practical if you were going to beat a man up, which was what she hoped for.

Caprice hoped for a cash settlement and clearing him out of her life. Out of the town she did not hope for. There were limits. This was something of a business trip to her, albeit a crucial one.

Birdie, the most theologically inclined, then handed round cups of hot herbal tea (peppermint and camomile mixed) to calm the nerves, suggested a short period of meditation to strengthen the spirit, then a prayer to the Great Earth Goddess for support, but Caprice wanted to get on.

Birdie was disappointed, she had begun to suspect that the Goddess was herself, that they were as one; she had been granted a touch of the divine. One knew it was distributed around.

'Come on,' said Caprice. 'Time's passing.'

Unshriven, they set out. Birdie drove, it was her car and she insisted. Caprice was a chancy driver and Winifred was mad today. 'I'm not insured for another driver,' she said. She turned the corner out of Merrywick.

Winifred put a gentle but restraining hand on Birdie's arm. 'Before we go I must feed my cat. Benedict cannot bear to be hungry.'

'Oh, forget the cat.' Caprice was impatient to be off.

'Pain for Benedict is the same as pain for me,' said Winifred. By which she meant: And I shall soon see there is some pain for you, too. She was the only one of them whose dooms occasionally worked.

'Oh rubbish, you spoil that cat. Let him starve.' Not that he would, great lump, enough fat on him to stand a siege. Birdie jerked her arm away.

'You try being a cat for a bit and see how you like it.' Winifred's eyes rested as coldly on Birdie as Benedict's own pale green gaze might have done. Birdie felt an uneasy movement inside her, just as her namesakes might have done at the sight of a cat.

Caprice slumped in the back seat, moving her long legs

uncomfortably. Packed in with her was a plastic sack inside which was a hammer, a chisel and a poker. And a spade, just in case. 'Let her feed the cat if she must. It's not much out of our way.'

'I'm driving the car,' said Birdie, 'and I say not.'

She swung the car across the junction, narrowly missing a car that was proceeding in the opposite direction. The driver hooted, Birdie hooted back.

'Ben,' said Winifred. 'Ben, Ben, Ben.'

Quarrelling, they drove on.

The door beside the jeweller's shop in Elm Street still had a streak of what might have been blood on it, the brass plate with J. Fox inscribed was even more unpolished, since two more days had weathered it. J. Fox did not care about the appearance of his door.

'Ring the bell,' commanded Birdie.

Caprice was already doing so. No one came. She rang again.

'He's not going to come.'

'I'll try the knocker, while you ring the bell.'

They stood there, one of them ringing the bell and the other banging the knocker.

'He can't be there,' said Birdie, between knocks.

'He's there, I feel he is there,' said Winifred. She had her eye pressed to the letterbox. 'I'm trying to see. Go on knocking.'

The jeweller appeared from his shop to demand angrily what was going on.

'I've got a young couple in here trying to choose an engagement ring. How can they do that with all this banging and shouting?'

'Be good for them, I should think.' Caprice stopped ringing. 'Give them a taste of the future, what married life's really like.'

'Are you married to that chap Fox, then?'

'Of course not.'

'Then stop all this racket.'

130

Birdie kept her hand on the knocker. 'Is Mr Fox inside, do you know?'

The jeweller said, 'Everyone's after him these days. Weeks and weeks when he could be dead for all I know, now three lots of ladies after him in as many days.'

'Three?' Birdie was surprised. 'Who were they?'

'I don't know.' He started to return to his shop. 'We weren't introduced. One the other day, and another one just before you. That one didn't make the noise you lot are making.'

'Is Mr Fox there?'

'Yes, I just told you. He's in and out. Here now, saw him go in with her.'

That was it, all the information he was parting with. He disappeared into his shop, with a quick movement managing to circumvent the young couple who were on the point of departure.

Caprice said, 'Be interesting to know who he's got in there with him.'

'Can we get in round the back?' Birdie stepped off into the street, assessing the situation. There seemed to be a side passage leading to the back of the block. It was presumably where cars were parked.

'Oh, do let's.' Winifred clapped her hands. 'Break in.' She shouldered the plastic sack, and the spade. 'I feel he is there, he is hearing us, he wants us to come in.'

Caprice gave her friend and enemy a sour look. She found Winifred on the other-worldly kick very irritating.

Birdie tried to take the spade; Winifred was handling it in such an aggressive way people would look. 'If he knew what we had in mind for him, he shouldn't.'

'He does, he does,' said Winifred with a triumphant shout. She disappeared round the corner of the passage.

The other two followed.

The local constable on the beat who was cycling slowly down the road saw the party as they hurried into the passage.

Wonder what that lot were up to? But they looked respectable ladies, the sort who might know your mother, so he pedalled on. He had no notion what he was watching. Witches rampant.

Josh Fox heard the ladies scrabbling at his back door. It sounded like scrabbling to him. From where he was it was more like a scrabble than a bang or a rattle. Mouse noises, he thought.

He had heard the noises at the front door also, but distantly.

Now he picked up voices, possibly one he recognised. The voices ceased and the scrabblings started again as though the mice were trying to get through the door.

Not mice, of course, mice did not try to get in through a door. People did.

As the noise seemed to get fainter, as if the mice, who were not mice, of course, but mice people, were giving up, he wished they would get in.

Get this business over, one way or another.

Chapter Twelve

In Alexandria Road on that same Tuesday the police team had shrunk. Another major inquiry, this time involving one of the Royal Household, had hit the beleaguered area, already burdened with two other important cases. Somehow the killing of a woman in her own home, although presenting fascinating aspects, now seemed of less importance.

Not to those working on it, of course.

'Damn,' said Dolly Barstow to Inspector Fred Elman, who had looked into the hall to impart the news. 'No one likes dogs better than I do, although I'm not all that fond of corgis. But to have three of the team called off is more than I can bear.'

'A bomb threat always has to be taken seriously,' said Elman. 'Even if it's to the kennels. And it wasn't nice for the dog-walker to be threatened with a gun.'

A member of the Household, walking a clutch of small dogs, had been threatened in the Park by a man with a gun who had then run off, either with, or followed by, the dogs. Next day there had been a telephone threat to bomb the kennels.

'How many dogs have been stolen?' asked Dolly gloomily.

'We don't know if they've been stolen. They may just have run off when their walker was attacked. Miss Anketell says they did.'

'Then they'll come back. Dogs always do.' If they liked their home, and this lot must do. Could they hope to find a better?

'They haven't done yet. And there is anxiety in the Household.' He added respectfully, 'Thank goodness the

133

dogs were being walked and not out with HM. It does happen, you know. Pops out the back door without a word to anyone and exercises them in the Park. It's very worrying.'

'You were lucky there.'

'Yes, everyone' – everyone who counted, he meant, seeing that Windsor had been as crowded as usual with inhabitants and tourists – 'was in London yesterday.'

So as a result of all this, the team in Alexandria Road was reduced by three, with the threat of another reduction if the highly secret case which Superintendent Father was embroiled in took him to Spain, as it might.

'Nothing much is happening here, is it?' said Elman. 'Face it, you're just filling in routine.'

He had gone through all the files, and read all the reports, speedily but carefully, he was a careful man.

He produced his summing up. 'In my experience, crimes like this have one answer: the motive is personal hatred. And it has to be a man. Sort through her past and pick out the right man and you're home and dry. I don't say it's the man Fox, although I think it could be.'

It was obvious that his solution was going to be different from Dolly Barstow's and different again from Charmian Daniels's. He was sure the killer was a man who was filled with anger; Dolly still had a feeling that one of the women had killed Vivien, although the blood groupings were a problem here, but a female revenge killing was how she saw the picture; and Charmian was forming a different picture altogether, one which took in aspects of both the Elman and Barstow solutions.

'Look for a man,' advised Elman. 'The obvious answer is often the right one. And routine, just as I said. You might dislike it but that's how you get results.'

Dolly had proof of this a few minutes after Inspector Elman left, still looking thoughtful about dogs and saying that he was a Boxer man himself.

A routine enquiry she had set in train, produced its result. Dolly was pleased. She thought it was interesting, might not be important, but she thought it would open things up.

She looked forward to telling Charmian. 'She'll like that info. Perhaps I don't like it very much myself but the truth is worth having.'

It explained a lot, too, about Mr Josh Fox.

Perhaps it did not make him more likeable, but it certainly made him more understandable as the warlock of Merrywick.

'And how mad those ladies will be if they ever find out. Kill him, I should think, if they could.'

And they would find out, she thought, possibly had already, because information always got around in the end. Let a piece of news about a person surface once and it took on a life of its own, rapidly moving and expanding until it was everywhere. Oh yes, they would find out.

She looked at her watch. Any minute now, she thought. Charmian would arrive first, and then Mr Josh Fox, alias Teddy Elder, would arrive to be confronted.

Charmian walked in somewhat late and full of apologies. 'I had trouble with Muff. The black cat Benedict, Winifred Eagle's cat, pushed through the kitchen window and ate Muff's food. There was a bit of a fight. I wish Miss Eagle would feed her own cat.'

She looked round the room.

'Josh Fox not here yet?'

Dolly shook her head. 'Not much over time. Might be the traffic. Anyway, I want to talk first, come into my cubby hole.' She had contrived a private place for herself in a screened-off alcove. Years of college life and working in libraries, three to a table, had made Dolly value a private work area. As she led the way, she said, 'Any idea what he is going to tell you?'

Charmian shook her head. 'Not much. I'm guessing.' She looked around. A neat table with a polished top, two wire baskets full of papers, a telephone, and a small lap-top computer. 'Nice little place you've made here . . . Something about himself, I think.'

'Good guessing.'

Dolly pushed a sheet of paper, a print-out from the main computer. 'Remember the red Cortina? A car of that type and with a very similar registration number came up as belonging to an Edward Elder in Sunbury. That didn't mean anything to me, but it rang a bell with the WDC doing the check.'

'Get on with it. I want to hear before Fox gets here.'

'She knew the name Elder. Ted Elder. She had heard of him as a detective working in the Met. He left. Voluntarily, she thought, but there might have been some trouble behind it. She rang up a friend.'

Charmian waited, she thought she could guess what was coming.

'Ted Elder bought a private detective agency. The contact didn't know the name, but knew that it was in Slough.'

'Josh Fox,' said Charmian. 'He's a private detective.' So was that why he was hanging about the house in Slough where Denise Flaxon lived? 'I'll be asking him some loaded questions about why and whom.'

Josh Fox, real name Teddy Elder. She ought to have guessed his trade. And if he'd been in the Met it explained why she had the idea she had seen him somewhere. No doubt she had done.

'He's going to tell you something, remember?'

'I can't wait.' Something about his work, who he was watching, who had paid him?

Dolly moved the pens around on her desk and looked at the clock.

Charmian stood up. 'What's the time? The sooner he comes now the better. He's late, where is he?'

While she was waiting, she sat reading all the day's reports that were gradually coming to rest on Dolly's desk. Taking Charmian's hint, Dolly had requested and got a report by what she called 'a City expert' on both the Cay-Cay organisation and their neighbour across the road in the glass building.

Cay-Cay was a PR agency of some reputation with another office in New York. There was nothing here for her.

But the report on the other business was more interesting.

The firm whose logo EL had attracted her, Charmian's, attention in Hatton was a large organisation with many and diverse activities. They had recently been on the acquisition trail and had been buying up estate agents, grouping them together in a chain called HOMELINE. Bloods, the old established estate agents in Merrywick, was one of their latest buys which accounted for it still using its own name.

'Have you read this?' she asked, laying the report in front of Dolly.

'No, I was just about to.'

'Read it. I was right,' said Charmian triumphantly. 'There is a link here. Vivien Charles met someone from that office across the road in Hatton Woods. Perhaps in the wine bar, perhaps just parking her car, and that someone might have become her lover, and might have suggested where she lived.'

'That's just guessing.'

'You start with guessing,' said Charmian.

She had noticed before that when one break came in an investigation, others swiftly followed. The trick was to tie disparate pieces of information together and make a picture of them.

Anything might come out. You could liken it to an original solution to a piece of research, an answer which would have been unguessable when you started out.

'How's Fred Elman?' she asked absently.

'You've just missed him. Laying down the law as usual, but quietly. He always thinks he knows all the answers. Of course, he's pretending to himself that you don't exist and are not doing anything here at all.' Dolly added philosophically, but tactfully, to herself, 'For which you can't blame him.'

'Do you know,' said Charmian suddenly, taking up the subject hitherto untouched between them, 'I haven't thought about my wretched hand for days.' She flexed her wrist.

'Must be getting better.'

'I get by, typing with one hand. I may never get back

to using two.' It was uttered in a light, lively tone which reflected how she felt.

'That's recovery,' thought Dolly. 'She's nearly well now. I must tell Kate.' Aloud, she said, 'Just got a few notes to read. Forgive me, will you?'

Charmian waited for Josh Fox, who was probably Teddy Elder, to keep his appointment. She fidgeted around.

'He's not going to come. Damn him.'

Dolly lifted her head from her work; she had been thinking the same herself for some time. 'Doesn't look like it.'

Charmian hung around for a little while longer, then when the man did not come, she left to go back to Maid of Honour Row where Kate might have reappeared.

Kate was out, but Muff was waiting for her.

After the coven, or as Birdie preferred, the committee, had banged fruitlessly on both the back and front door of the premises in Elm Street, they withdrew to consider matters.

With silent accord they went to the coffee shop in The Parade. A table in the window accommodated them in comfort, with a spare chair for the bag of equipment. The spade got them some curious glances but no comment was made. Or not to their faces.

Caprice ordered coffee and carried over the cups – there was no waitress service in The Oak Pantry. As she sat down, the girl behind the coffee machine said to her colleague who was buttering scones, 'Think they're digging for gold?'

'If they find any round here, they'll be lucky.'

Birdie complained to Caprice about the quality and the price of the coffee. 'And it's not even hot.'

'Go and tell them yourself, then.'

Winifred drained her coffee before it got any colder and interrupted them.

'You know I'm sure he was there. I think I saw a foot when I peeped through the letterbox.'

'Standing there listening to us?' Caprice was willing to believe he might do that. It was what she would do herself.

138

'No,' said Winifred thoughtfully. 'Didn't look like that sort of a foot.'

'You are a fool, Winifred Eagle.' Birdie was irritated, as she always was when Winifred started to get what she called 'silly'.

Winifred picked up the spade. 'Drink your coffee. I think we ought to go back and break in. After all, it's what we meant to do, isn't it?'

'I don't remember putting it like that.'

'It's one thing we can do. The other thing we can do is to go to the police.'

'Talk sense.'

'Or we can go home.'

When Charmian walked into her sitting room at Maid of Honour Row she found there was a message for her on her answering machine. She listened.

'This is—' began a voice, then stopped.

Charmian waited. Very soon she realised that nothing else was coming. The message had ended before it had rightly begun.

Like many police officers Charmian had had her share of strange telephone messages from angry, lost, or crazed persons. People in trouble, people in pain, she'd had them all. But this one seemed different.

It had sounded like Josh Fox. Something wrong with his voice, though.

The young police constable on the bike who had seen the trio of women entering the passageway off Elm Street was surprised to see the same group going down it again.

He dismounted from his bike, found a safe place to leave it (even policemen have to watch their property), and approached the alley on foot.

He could not see them, so they must have gone round the corner into the area of garages and parking. On night duty, it was one of the places he checked. During the day there were usually people around and he did not have to worry so much.

He hesitated, all seemed quiet, such respectable-looking women, even if one of them was carrying a spade. For gardening, perhaps. He had once had his card marked by the Sergeant for dealing harshly with a group of women who turned out to have been on their way to a harmless gardening festival and not planting a bomb at all. He didn't want the same thing to happen again.

He turned back to where he had left his bike. A youth in torn jeans was examining it with apparent interest.

'Hi you!' He hurried off.

Winifred said, 'Give it a bang. Go at it harder, or we'll never get in.'

Birdie, who was trying to force the back door to J. Fox's, recognised that Winifred was in one of her wilder moods, it had been coming on all day. For longer, if she was honest with herself.

'I'm trying to be quiet. We want to get in quietly and confront him.'

'Money or your life,' said Winifred gleefully.

'It's not just money we're after,' said Caprice. 'We just want any files he's been building up on us and any photographs. Adverse publicity could have a very bad effect on Twickers.' Besides bringing the police to look deeper into what she dealt in there. 'Be careful, Birdie, he's bigger than us.'

'That's why we brought the poker. But he can't be there.'

'He's there,' said Winifred. 'I feel he is there.'

The door, which had been locked but not bolted, suddenly gave before her.

'I don't feel so brave any more,' said Winifred. 'I wanted to kill him, bury him with my little spade, but now . . . I feel different. Oh so different. How do you feel, Birdie?'

Birdie did not answer. She was realising with a shock that she, Alice Peacock, had just broken into a house. Surely white witches should be above such behaviour? Or do it by prayer? But her prayers hadn't worked for some time now, perhaps never would again. Oh, I'm a sinner, she thought,

I shall have to find someone to confess to. I wonder if Father O'Flynn would understand. He was several religions back, but she had found him sympathetic.

Caprice had pushed past her into the narrow hall, which ran from the front door to the back door with a staircase leading off it. Inside was surprisingly dark for such a bright day.

In the hall was a wall telephone which appeared to be hanging free, as if just dropped. She did not replace it. Some instinct warned her to touch nothing.

Winifred and Birdie followed her slowly, getting their bearings as their eyes got used to the dark. There was a shape, a darkness within the dark. A solid shadow. There was a smell as well.

Someone was lying slumped at the bottom of the stairs with his feet towards the front door, blood and the by-products of his death agonies leaking out around him.

The policeman had recovered his bike and was about to continue his progress when he saw one of the women run out of the passage that ran between the two blocks of buildings. She was waving, and probably crying as well.

He went towards her. 'Now calm down, madam, and tell me what's up. Dead? He may not be, let's go and have a look.'

He followed Birdie down the passage, round the corner into the yard and then into the house where two other women were standing, one holding a spade and the other a poker. A chisel lay on the floor.

He did not ask them how they had got into the building, that would have to come later.

At the bottom of the stairs, almost as if he had been trying to reach the front door but hadn't been able to make it, was a man. Blood stained his shirt front and formed a pool on the floor. A knife lay by his side.

'Yes, he's dead,' said the young constable. 'Stabbed.'

Chapter Thirteen

The report came into the temporary Incident Room in Alexandria Road about the middle of the morning on Wednesday, whence it soon found its way to Sergeant Barstow's desk. It was read almost at once by Dolly Barstow who sent a copy round to Charmian by a messenger. So there was no delay. Dolly had a patch of eczema on one cheek that was worrying her.

The report was dated Wednesday, a.m., and had been sent out by the Slough CID.

The body of a man, identified provisionally as Josh Fox, was discovered in the hall of a house in Elm Street, The Parade, Slough, at approximately 3.30 p.m. yesterday afternoon. The discovery was made by three women. (Names attached.) There is some doubt about identification. The man worked as Josh Fox which was the trade name of his detective agency only. He was carrying papers which suggest his real name was Ted or Edward Elder.

He appeared to have been stabbed in the neck and abdomen. It is estimated that he had been dead less than an hour when discovered. Attack might have taken place some few hours before.

There were signs of earlier injuries on the deceased's face. Height five feet eleven. Weight stripped twelve stone. Features about dental and details of fingerprints will follow.

Information about this man is requested by Superintendent Arbat, Slough CID. Also any details about the three women.

Scrawled in his own handwriting, Superintendent Peter Arbat, who had met Dolly and, as he put it to himself, fancied her like mad, had added the following note:

I think this might be of interest to you. I hear you have your eye on this chap. He looked to have been in a fight. If you know anything about him, we would like to know. Also any news about the women would be helpful. Who are these old birds, do you hatch them specially in Merrywick? Keep in touch.

He had attached two copies of a photograph of Josh Fox, otherwise Ted Elder. Some cosmetic work must have been done on him, since he was clearly, but not too clearly, dead at the time.

Dolly, who knew Pete Arbat, and also knew his reputation, grinned. She had, as he had probably guessed, taken deliberate evasive action on the occasion of the New Year Police Ball. But that did not mean she was not interested. Only that she was thinking about it.

We might be able to tell you something, Buster, she thought. Ted Elder had been a policeman, did you know that? Clearly Superintendent Arbat had not known. Sloppy policework there and she would enjoy not pointing out this remissness but letting him do that for himself when she passed the information along in due course. As she would do. He would be aware of her silent criticism and she would have the pleasure of not showing it.

That put Dolly one ahead in the game.

And with luck, because Peter Arbat was a sharp observer, especially of women, she would keep from him the pain that photograph of the dead man had given her. Her eczema began to feel better.

Charmian came round to see for herself as soon as she got the message. She had in the interval been active herself.

She had set up an interview at EL House in Hatton

143

Woods, calling upon all the influence at her command to get entrance.

Because it had not been easy. EL House guarded itself against intruders. Her own position and the nature of her enquiry saw her in, but she needed to prepare herself first.

Her City informant told her that the boss, Leonard Eden, had had a bad experience with the press on his way up and now did not give interviews or allow his staff to do so. Instant dismissal followed any breach of this rule.

'Secretive cove,' the City Editor of *The Globe* had said.

'You know him?'

'Met him once. You never see him around at the popular watering holes. Not his style. Said to live a solid domestic life in one of the richer suburbs.'

'Do you know where?'

Harry Jarvis thought about it. 'I'll ask around. Surrey somewhere, I think.'

'I've met him once myself.'

'Bet you didn't get much out of him.'

'Well, we weren't talking,' said Charmian, remembering the interview in Bloods. 'I was more interested in someone else at the time.'

'He may live round your way.'

'Yes,' agreed Charmian, remembering how Surrey and Berkshire joined near Windsor. 'Probably does. Seemed to take a local interest. Thanks for your help.'

'Well, I wish you luck with them. Closed-up lot at EL. If you pick up anything interesting you might let me know.'

The conversation ended with an invitation from him to lunch or, if she couldn't spare the time, for a drink. He liked Charmian. Also, it was as well to keep in with the police.

The call from Dolly to Charmian came just at the right time. She was shocked but not totally surprised. Somehow Josh Fox had been a worrying man. Trouble hung around him.

'I wondered where he was. Never thought of death, though. Just that he'd changed his mind.'

'Looks as though someone didn't want him to talk to you.'

'Possibly. But it doesn't have to be that. They may just have wanted him dead. Dead men tell no secrets.' And don't try blackmail. There was that hint of trouble behind Ted Elder's premature retirement.

Dolly said, 'I'm in touch with the Slough police, and, of course, it's their body and their case, but in view of our interest we are co-operating.' To a certain extent, she added to herself. 'They will be letting me check over his records, so we know who his clients were. That's important, don't you think?'

'Very important,' said Charmian. 'Very helpful if we find a name we know there. But people do use aliases.'

'He'd check on that. Be the first thing he'd do.'

'I agree,' said Charmian. 'But he wouldn't necessarily keep a record for us.'

'I expect it was that he wanted to tell you.'

'Could be.'

Charmian left a message for Kate, who had now been absent for some days and about whom one might have worried if it had not been such a characteristic piece of behaviour, and drove round to Alexandria Road. She moved at such speed that it took her less than ten minutes.

By which time Dolly knew that three sets of callers had been after Josh Fox in the last few days of his life and been observed by the jeweller.

Charmian was one such caller, as she said at once. 'I was there. Spoke to the jeweller. He'll know my face. But I didn't see Josh Fox.' Or Ted Elder as they now ought to call him. 'I never thought of going round the back. But I don't believe he was there. Not at that time . . . I wish I'd known he was looking for me.'

'Don't we all?'

Ted Elder most of all, probably, in those long minutes before he died. The preliminary pathologist's report did not make pretty reading. He had been stabbed several times, one wound severing the main artery in the stomach. Yet he had not died straight away. From the marks on his hands it looked as though he had tried to drag himself to the door as he felt his life ebbing away. But he hadn't had the strength left in him to do it.

'Must have heard the three women at the front door and tried to get to them,' said Dolly; she felt a bit sick at the picture she was calling up. She had liked the man and thought he had liked her.

'But he didn't make it.' He had tried to telephone as well.

He had probably died while the witches were drinking their coffee down the road and quarrelling about whether to go back to his door or not.

'Those three were the last to call on him. And he certainly was dead by the time they got into the house.' Dolly herself would see to some very sharp questioning of the three women. 'I don't think they killed him, although I'd like to believe they could have done. But the other caller . . . well, it's the one in the middle we need to find.'

'Did the jeweller give a description?'

Dolly consulted her notes. It was a hot afternoon and she was sweating, the palms of her hands felt greasy. Charmian Daniels on the other hand looked cool and fresh.

'I don't know if you could call it a description. I wouldn't call him much of an observer and he'll make a hell of a poor witness if we ever get so far.' She pushed her notes across the table. 'Here, read for yourself while I get a drink of water.'

'Get one for me.'

'Or coffee? Not iced.' Probably not even really hot, they went in more for the pallidly warm stuff in the Incident Room here. Something to do with the coffee-maker not liking being moved, it seemed.

'No, water.'

That wouldn't be iced, either, but Dolly ran the tap until the water was cold, letting it pour over her wrists as well, while she watched Charmian read.

Charmian drank the water. 'Thanks. He says he saw the woman at the front door. He was going to his car to collect some goods and only saw her from the back.

He says she was a tallish, thin woman wearing jeans and a white shirt. When he came back she was gone . . . Do you think it really was a woman?'

'If you read on, you will see he also says she had a mane of bright red hair hanging down her back. Not many men like that. And not one we know.'

'We don't know a woman like that, either.'

'I expect Slough will find her,' said Dolly hopefully.

Charmian laughed. 'Perhaps the Josh Fox agency kept colour photographs of clients,' she suggested.

'Much more likely to keep photographs of people he was investigating.'

'I expect he did if he could get them. I would myself.' The camera was a great aid to detection, Charmian thought.

'Get Slough to look, then.'

Dolly nodded. 'I'll do that.' She took a deep breath. The gods must be on the side of Superintendent Peter Arbat, Dolly decided; they would be in touch.

'I wouldn't mind interviewing that jeweller myself,' said Charmian, who hadn't liked the man. 'Can anyone be that vague?'

'You weren't wearing jeans yourself, were you?' Dolly looked at Charmian's red hair.

'No, I was not. Not me. Some other female.'

Dolly said gloomily, 'This case is sprouting figures like a plant. First a couple of men, now a woman who might just be a man.'

'I'm going to find one of the men if I can. And I may flush out the man-woman in the process.'

'Good for you,' said Dolly. 'Let me know who you find.'

Charmian got up. 'You'll be the first. Meanwhile, I suppose you'll be talking to the local coven?'

'As soon as Slough lets me. I gather they want first go. Of course Peacock and Co were questioned straight away by the local CID sergeant, and then held for more questioning. They'll have been washed clean of information. I don't expect to get much out of them.'

'At least you can find out why they went there.'

'Looking for revenge, I expect. They must have found out about the true nature of Josh Fox's interest in them.'

'But that's something to think about in itself, isn't it? Why was he watching them, and who had paid him to do it. Because he must have been paid. Think about it, Dolly.'

'Check the records,' said Dolly slowly. 'Ought to be something there. We'll have to hope he kept careful records.'

'Oh, he did, I'm sure. He was a professional. But he may have used some form of coding. Just for his use only.'

Before she left Charmian asked for one of the photographs of Josh Fox who was really Ted Elder. 'Just something I'm thinking about,' she said.

Charmian sat in her car and thought.

She realised, even if Dolly did not, that with this second murder the situation had changed.

Dolly Barstow would be crowded out of the investigation. Inspector Elman and Superintendent Father would take over. They couldn't afford not to now that Peter Arbat was involved; rank would have to speak to rank.

Her own position would alter. Because of who she was and her position in London she would be tolerated, she would still be a 'special adviser', an *ad hoc* role to be accepted and passed over as much as possible. But she would not be welcome.

Dolly Barstow had been allowed to manage what seemed like an ordinary unsolvable little case not likely to bring promotion nearer to the likes of Fred Elman, while Superintendent Father, absorbed in matters more sensitive politically, had been willing to delegate. He usually was willing to delegate, it was both his strength and his weakness.

Charmian knew both men, and sympathised with their workload in a busy force with special responsibilities because of the town they protected, but she could see that now they would start to be more active in what had turned into a double murder.

Unless you believed in coincidence and thought that Ted Elder had been killed in connection with something quite other than the murder of Vivien Charles, just at the time when he had got ready to talk to Charmian.

Charmian did not believe this judgement.

What did she think of the case herself now? She tried to assemble her thoughts.

To begin with, how did she feel about it? Because feelings counted. They were clues to the inner thought processes.

One thing she felt was excited. That was unexpected and meant that underneath she sensed she knew the answer.

That wasn't such a surprise to her as it might have been to Dolly.

Alexandria Road was at no time a pretty road. As well as the church hall now housing the Incident Room it was also home to several small factories and workshops, some of which looked as though they had been left around since the Industrial Revolution. The first one, the one when the early Celts discovered iron. It was a bit of Windsor discreetly hidden from the tourists.

Cars lined the street on both sides so that lorries hooted and disputed the rights of passage with each other as they tried to get through. It was on a bus route as well which made life even more difficult.

Charmian looked through her windscreen. Someone was coming down the road, sticking bits of paper on the car windows. Not a traffic warden, as might have been expected from the number of illegally parked cars on double yellow lines, but a boy. Tall, thin and scruffy. He was setting about his job with less than total effort, jamming the papers anywhere that caught his eye. Or didn't catch his eye – one or two pieces were distributed at random while he gazed upon a young girl passing by. Several papers were already fluttering aloft in the strong wind.

There was a look about the papers that reminded Charmian of something.

She waited until he came up to her, then she wound the window down. 'What is it you're doing?'

He stared at her, speech clearly not being his chosen means of communication.

'Selling something,' he said, after a bit.

'What though?'

'Dunno.'

'Here give one to me.'

She grabbed one of the advertisements from his limp hand. It came away so readily that she felt the whole pile could be hers for the asking.

'Have as many as you like.'

He had a satchel slung over one shoulder full of more supplies, but he looked ready to abandon the lot at any moment.

Perhaps he thought she was making a collection.

'Thanks, one is enough.'

While she was reading, he sat down on the kerb and lit a cigarette. 'Rotting my lungs,' he said conversationally.

Charmian read:

SELLING YOUR HOME?

SELL THROUGH US

HOMELINE

YOUR NEW LOCAL AGENCY

FASTEST AND BEST

'What's it say? Don't do much reading myself.'

The advertisement was printed on bright yellow paper. Round the edges, in a kind of formalised border, the logo EL was patterned.

'It's about selling your house.'

'I thought it might be,' he said.

'Why did you think that?'

'Usually is,' he said simply. 'Or about moving your furniture. One or the other.'

'Do you work for these people?'

'No. I just go to the printer's shop and pick up the bundles. He pays me.'

'I thought money must come into it,' said Charmian drily.

'Why you asking these things, lady?'
'Just wondered. Not much of a job.'
'All I got.'

Clearly feeling that something more was, or might be, demanded of him, and willing to oblige, he said, 'Are you selling your home, miss?'

'No.'

Charmian wound down her window. She did not return her advertisement, she did not wish to add to the disappointment he so clearly felt already.

As she drove off, he was back at his lackadaisical work. Not with any energy but with a fair persistence, about every third advertisement getting into position. As he said, it was all he had and he got paid.

Charmian wondered if his employers searched him for undelivered advertisements before he got the cash.

In spite of this interruption, she discovered her thoughts had clarified.

Vivien Charles had been stabbed with a knife taken from her own kitchen. Around her had been arranged various unpleasant articles associated with witchcraft. Traces of two types of unusual blood groups had been found in the kitchen. Vivien was the source of one type of blood, her murderer may have been the source of the other.

Only may have been, since there was evidence that someone had been in that house in Dulcet Road after the killing. Further, that someone appeared to have had a key.

That key could have come from Bloods, from whom Vivien had rented her house on a short-term lease, and who appeared to be casual about keys.

Bloods now belonged to HOMELINE which itself belonged to this corporation EL.

One more fact: Vivien was pregnant when she died. She could have met her lover in the street where she worked. The girls with whom she had worked at Cay–Cay had thought so. Charmian thought so too.

The EL was in that same street. Just across the way, in fact.

There were trailers, odd facts, which she hadn't worked

in yet. Such as what had happened to Vivien Charles that had caused the malformation of her child? An infection, a natural accident of life, or a shock?

If a shock, then what shock and delivered by what instrument?

Another fact: the death of Ted Elder, working as Josh Fox, who had been watching the witches, was in there somewhere. She suspected he had tried blackmail, regretted it and tried to contact her.

She must have seen him somewhere, at some London gathering, and he had seen her. Perhaps found reason to trust her.

There were some things she might never find out, but she meant to find out about Josh Fox. His memory needed either redeeming or condemning, and she wanted to find out which. He deserved that much.

She was driving faster and faster as the thoughts poured out. She had also taken the wrong way round, so that she was caught in a lot of busy traffic that was heading towards Slough town centre. Clearly it was Woodstock Close for her first call and the EL building in Hatton Woods second.

In Woodstock Close there was more activity than was usual at this hour in the afternoon, especially on a Wednesday when a midweek lull seemed to occur. It was a day when the milkman did not call, when the postman appeared to give the area only one delivery of letters and when even the huge Alsatian dog that promenaded the streets, a menace to pedestrians and motorists alike, was taken off by his owner for his weekly defleaing at the local veterinary surgery. This had to be done weekly because owing to his size and his temper it was very difficult to work on him for more than five harried minutes. That it was done at all was to prevent a divorce between the co-owners, one of whom loved the dog, fleas and all, and the other of whom hated him. Neither could control him. Lately they could only go to bed when the dog said Yes.

But this Wednesday saw Miss Jessamon already pretending

152

to clean her windows while Ferdy Schmidt was watching at his half-open door. Nor were they alone in this, other residents in other houses in the street were on the look-out as well. Window boxes were being watered and gardens that usually never saw a spade were being turned over.

The reason for this alertness was the TV film crew assembling itself in the street. It was believed they were filming for a commercial. Rumour had it that it was to advertise a new washing powder, another rumour spoke of a building society. But the most popular part of the rumour was that they would be recruiting locals for a crowd scene.

Miss Jessamon went into the front garden to check if her windows were as clean as they should be, and met Denise Flaxon on her way out of the house. Denise was carrying the neat black bag which she usually took to work. Elysium Creams supplied a similar bag but Denise preferred to use her own.

'Afternoon, dear,' said Miss Jessamon.

'Good afternoon.' Denise put on her dark sunglasses against the glare of the street.

'You off to work, then?'

'I've got to cover an area way out of town. I'm going today so I can make an early start tomorrow.' Denise smoothed her hair where the side of the spectacles had disarranged it. She was always very neat, her hair particularly groomed and precise.

'You do work hard, dear, we don't see much of you.'

'I haven't been doing very well,' said Denise with a sigh. 'I'm afraid I may have to give up my franchise with Elysium. I have to renew it soon anyway and I don't know if I can afford it. Or if they'll take me on again. My sales haven't been much.'

Miss Jessamon made sympathetic noises. She had bought a pot of Elysium night cream herself to help Denise and very pretty it looked on her dressing table, much too pretty to open and use.

'You see what we've got in the street?'

153

Denise glanced down the road to where the film crew were assembling outside a big van. 'I do. Isn't it a nuisance? I shall have a job getting my car out. I'm just going to put this case in the car and get one more case down and then I'm off.'

'I'll keep an eye on your place, dear,' volunteered Miss Jessamon happily. 'I mean with persons watching the house, who knows what might happen.'

'There hasn't been any more of that, has there?'

'No,' said Miss Jessamon, who regretted it. 'I would have known if there had. But do you ever get the feeling that there's someone in your place? Someone who shouldn't have been there?'

Denise, who had indeed had this feeling but who had discounted it as imagination on her part, stared at her neighbour. The old bird must be psychic or something.

Miss Jessamon put out a thin hand to gently touch the other woman. 'I heard you crying the other night, my dear. I am sorry. Let me know if I can help.'

Charmian had to search for somewhere to park when she drove up. Most of the road seemed blocked by a large van with appendages of cables and accessories. SOUTH TV was proclaimed in large letters on the side of the van.

She tucked her car away, then walked towards the house where she could see Miss Jessamon watering a plant in the front garden.

On her way she passed a dark-haired woman hiding behind tinted glasses who was just getting into her car.

Miss Jessamon was pleased to see Charmian. Less pleased perhaps than on a normal quiet day when she had nothing to watch, but glad to welcome her.

'See what's going on in our street? Hive of activity, aren't we?' She opened the gate to let Charmian in. 'They're going to use some of us in the crowd scene.'

'Really? I should keep out of the way if I were you. You don't want to see your face flickering away on the TV screen, do you?'

154

Flo Jessamon looked at her as if she couldn't believe what she was hearing. 'Some people might not, but I do.'

Ferdy Schmidt had heard voices and came out of the front door. 'Oh, it's you.' He was disappointed. No TV prospects there. In any case, he didn't like police officers, even good-looking female ones.

'Can I come into the house?' Charmian asked. 'I want to ask you something.'

'Of course,' said Flo. 'My sitting room. With pleasure.'

'Both of you.'

'Glad to.' Flo was a generous soul and willing to share this small happiness with Ferdy Schmidt, who had been very down in the mouth lately.

She led the way in, followed by Charmian and Dr Schmidt, who smelt strongly of garlic with a hint of paprika. Then she turned with a radiant smile. 'Out with it, then. Open up.'

'You remember the man or men you two saw watching the house? Of course you do. I expect you both have good visual memories?'

'I have,' agreed Flo Jessamon. She was sure she did have. Never forgot a face. Names, yes. Faces, no.

Ferdy contented himself with a small nod. He wasn't going to lay a claim to anything until he saw where it led. It had been his rule in life. Never volunteer, and if possible hide.

Charmian drew out the doctored photograph of Josh Fox – Ted Elder. She offered it first to Ferdy Schmidt.

Ferdy made a production of it. First he handed it back to her. 'Wait.' Then he took a spectacle case from his breast pocket. Then he withdrew his spectacles and then he took out a large white handkerchief with which to polish them. This took a little time before he had them clean enough; he held them up several times to check, frowning as he did so.

'Hurry up, Ferdy, do.'

He ignored Flo's impatience. One last twirl with the handkerchief and he was ready.

He took the photograph over to the window where he studied it in silence.

Flo rolled her eyes at Charmian. 'He sees better without them, anyway, as I know for a fact.'

'It's all right, Miss Jessamon,' said Charmian, her eyes on the man. She believed he had made a decision.

Ferdy handed the picture back. 'Yes, it is. This is the man I saw watching the house. Or I judge so.'

'Thank you. I thought you'd say that.'

Flo said, 'Now my turn.'

Silently Charmian handed the photograph over.

Flo, who had managed to get a good look earlier while Ferdy hung about, took no time at all. 'No, this is definitely not the man I saw. Definitely not.'

'Thank you,' said Charmian again. 'I felt sure that was the case.'

Ferdy said softly and sadly, 'That man there is dead, is he not? Yes, I thought so. One could not mistake the look.'

While this was going on, Dolly Barstow had made a decision. An interviewing job needed doing which she would like to have done for herself, but she knew that she was too busy. Many tasks here demanded her attention.

She considered whom she could send. In many ways she believed a man would be best, someone alert to atmosphere, intelligent but quiet. A man who might notice what other people did not.

She hadn't got many to choose from and not many like that, but she thought she knew one.

She strolled across the room. 'Know where Rewley is?' she demanded to the room.

Rewley was unique. Not many like George Rewley. Quite as it should be, some said.

Chapter Fourteen

One watcher dead and one man still to be looked for. This was in Charmian's mind as she drove away to the EL building in Hatton Woods. The traffic was heavy at this time of the day, mid afternoon and midweek, so that it was a slow drive, with cars and buses pushing at her on either side. She had to drive slowly.

This she did not mind, because she needed to think. She was aware that she was going to have to summon up all her nerve, call it cheek if you like, in the interviews she had ahead of her.

The magic password that would get her inside the glass building was not her own name and rank, nor the note from the Assistant Commissioner, but a card with a message on it from Alistair Brinkman, one of those mysterious and powerful City figures for whom doors are always opened. And this card she had only obtained because he was a friend of Humphrey Kent. She did not admire herself for using this form of influence but it seemed the time. Her own credentials would have got her in, the police do have powers, but tongues would not have been loosened. She had telephoned ahead to make sure of her reception.

The doors opened and closed behind her automatically; she had the strong feeling that it would have been difficult to get out of the EL building unless those inside chose to let you out. She observed that the doors had opened to let her in only because a well-dressed young woman behind a desk had nodded to a man in uniform who had pressed a button.

In front of Charmian was a bank of flowers, pale yellow and white, mixed with lots of greenery. No smell of living plants, however, such as you got in a conservatory, and yet they were not plastic flowers, only deadened by the air conditioning.

The elegant young person had her own private flower display on her desk, this too was yellow and white. Sitting behind her flowered embankment, with a well-controlled smile on her pretty face, the girl reminded Charmian of her cat Muff when waiting for a meal, ready to accept or spurn as the offering came up, prepared to scratch or purr as the occasion demanded.

Probably she herself fell below the standard of appearance required in this place. She had not dressed over-carefully that morning when she left the house in a hurry, and the events of the day had untidied her hair and chewed off any lipstick she might have applied. She had left behind her a sink of unwashed dishes and a cat, locked in and contemplating her own form of revenge.

There was a board in front of the flowers with 'Mary Fraser' written on it in gold. Charmian introduced herself to Mary Fraser who rose. 'Oh, Miss Daniels, yes. Would you follow me, please? There is a small reception room where you can talk to whomever you please. The head personnel officer, Mr Grink, will be coming down to see you.'

All preparations had been made for her welcome, thought Charmian, and the same to you, Mr Grink.

'Nice flowers,' she said, as they got into a lift which had its own small pot plant. 'I see it's yellow and white week. Do you do the arranging?'

Miss Fraser knew it was a joke and allowed Charmian to know that she knew a joke when she saw one, she gave her a gentle smile. 'An outside company comes in and does them. They decide the colours. They're into colourpower.'

The interview room, which was small but comfortable with a desk, two armchairs and the flowers, had no window.

Charmian, who had seen herself wandering about freely talking to all, realised she was to be tethered.

'But it doesn't matter as much as you might think,' said Charmian to Miss Fraser's back as the door closed behind her. 'Because I know where I am going.'

'Just a minute,' she called, producing a photograph. 'Do you know this face?'

No, Miss Fraser had never seen Vivien. Vivien had worked across the road, they were much the same age, but Mary Fraser did not know Vivien Charles.

An hour or so later, having passed this time in the company of Mr Grink who was remarkably similar in style to Miss Bridget O'Neill of Cay-Cay but with a higher gloss on him, so that Charmian felt there must be one role model they were both imitating, she had worked her way through a random selection of EL employees, of both sexes, varied ages, and from all departments.

Mr Grink sat with her as a kind of chaperone. At the end of the first hour she could see on his sophisticated face the comment that a junior CID officer could have conducted these interviews so what was a woman of her rank doing them for?

Mr Grink himself had studied the photograph of Vivien Charles and not known her. He knew about her murder though, and this knowledge, although unexpressed, was written all over his careful face as he examined the picture.

Charmian consulted the notes she had made. 'Can I speak to Jim Robertson again?'

'From the driving pool?' He gave Charmian the kind of bleached smile he reserved for suggestions he didn't much like the look of and pressed a button. He spoke into the telephone. 'Ask Jim to come up, will you?'

The telephone muttered back.

'As soon as he gets back, then.' To Charmian, Simon Grink said, 'He's gone out on an errand, I'm afraid.'

'I'll wait.'

'He might be some time.'

Charmian nodded, implying she would wait all day if she had to.

'Shall we have some tea or coffee while we wait?' Mr

159

Grink had resigned himself to more of Charmian. 'Shall we go along to our rest-room?'

So she was to be let out of prison? As they took another ride in yet another lift, Charmian asked, 'This is a newish building. How long has EL been in Hatton Woods?'

'About two years.'

Now she was getting used to the building she was aware of the air of prosperity it exuded. No expense spared. This idea was reinforced by the comfortable rest-room furnished in deep green leather. The tea too, when it came, was presented in good china. Apart from two young men sitting at a table before the window with a pile of papers between them, no one else was in the room, which did not look much used. Probably no one rested much in EL.

Jim Robertson was waiting for them when they got back, a small, stocky and now slightly anxious man. Why was he wanted again?

'I showed you this photograph before.'

'Yes, and I said I did not know her,' said Robertson quickly.

'What you actually said was: "Never spoke to her in my life."'

'Same thing.'

'Not really.'

They sat in silence for a minute, during which Jim Robertson looked from Charmian to Grink and then down to the floor. He shifted his feet uneasily.

'I'll let you off the hook by telling you what I think,' said Charmian. 'I think you are an honest man, Jim, who would like to tell the truth if he could.'

Jim's face slowly reddened.

'So you did the best you could. I don't think you have spoken to Vivien Charles, but you have seen her.'

He looked down at the floor and muttered something.

'Speak up.'

'I might have driven her.'

'Go on.'

160

'I do sometimes get asked to drive visitors around. In one of the company cars.'

Charmian looked at Simon Grink who nodded, he was beginning to show more and more tension.

'It would have to be someone in the top echelon who could ask,' he said.

Charmian turned to Jim Robertson. 'Where did you collect her?'

'The door here.'

'And where did you take her?' she asked.

He thought for a moment, but she guessed he knew the answer. 'Out Windsor way.'

'And at whose request?'

'I wouldn't know that, I wouldn't have to know. Just one of the bosses. I'd just get a call on the blower from one of the secretaries.'

Charmian looked again at Simon Grink who nodded. 'Could be.'

'One more thing, what age are the cars in the pool?'

'We change every year. This year's registration,' he said. 'G.'

'Thank you.'

She let Robertson go. As he left the room, she said, 'All the same, I think he knows who the boss figure was.'

Grink looked as if he might know too.

'I think it's time to see Mr Eden, don't you?'

'Mr Eden? . . . Oh, I don't know if . . .' he began.

Charmian stood up. 'Don't say it, Mr Grink, don't say it. Just show me the way.'

She managed to shed Mr Grink in the ante-room to the great man's office. She felt he was glad to melt away.

And yet Eden himself when she had been let into his room by his secretary, a straight-faced, grey-haired lady, was polite and gentle. A surprise.

As the room was also. Plainly the interior decorator had got into the room first and provided the sleek desk and matching chairs together with the sleek fall of silk curtains. The same hand had selected the two big pictures on opposite walls which might or might not be a Lowry and a Sidney Nolan, but all this had been disarranged and overlaid by the owner of the room.

He appeared to have created a comfortable clutter of papers, books and coffee cups. Across the room a bank of screens flashed quietly at intervals, but he seemed content to ignore them. His secretary shook her head and removed two cups and a mug as she went out.

He didn't smoke and he didn't like air conditioning. His jacket was off and hanging over a chair, and the window was open.

Also, there were no flowers. Either he did not like flowers or was allergic to them.

Leonard Eden, whose initials had certainly contributed to the name of his business, was tall, fair-skinned but without the deceiving tan so many business men seemed to find obligatory, and had allowed his faintly greying hair to develop a bald spot with no attempt to hide it. Charmian had known toupees worn for less.

She had seen him once already as he made a hurried departure from the estate agents in Merrywick, but probably he had not even noticed her presence that day. Then he had looked abstracted and busy, not someone she would take to. Now she was surprised to find herself liking him.

That he didn't remember her was apparent.

But he showed himself well briefed. He held out a friendly hand. 'Good afternoon, Chief Superintendent. Let's take those seats by the window, shall we?'

A view across the rooftops to Hatton Woods railway station looked more romantic from his eyrie than it had any right to do. A warm breeze came through the window, not smelling of flowers or trees as it might have done in Windsor, but of London traffic.

'Tea? Coffee? No, let's have a drink.' He went over to a small refrigerator which was not pretending to be an art deco cabinet but still managed to look dark and elegant. From it he took a bottle of white wine. 'Ice? Soda water?

162

Spoils the wine but makes a good drink . . . Alistair and I used to share an office years ago.'

That explained something, she thought.

'Thank you for giving me the freedom to talk to whom I wanted.'

'Did you find anything helpful?'

Charmian sipped her chilled and watered wine. 'Possibly. I think I did.'

'Ah. Good.'

He seemed relaxed, leaning back in the wide chair, letting the breeze blow over his face. A telephone rang briefly on his desk, then was quickly silenced from outside. He ignored the interruption, as Charmian felt he would always ignore what he did not want to be bothered with.

She had the idea that what she was seeing was a carefully composed appearance, a mask behind which the man hid himself. There were plenty such in the police and she had learnt that it covered up a good deal of emotion. Such men often had a soft centre.

'Grink show you round all right? He's a decent sort behind the bow-tie. Lost his wife last year. Childbirth. Still happens sometimes.'

The comment underlined something about Simon Grink, Charmian thought, and also about his boss that he had mentioned it. 'He did fine,' she said.

She held the photograph of Vivien Charles in her hands for a moment before showing it to him.

'This girl was murdered. Someone here knew her. Knew her well, I think.'

'Are you sure?'

'As sure as I can be of anything. And pretty sure I know who.'

He didn't rise to this comment but picked up the photograph and studied it silently. 'I can't help you. No.' And he handed back the photograph.

'I'm sorry about that.' Charmian stood up. 'I had a feeling you were going to be helpful.' She put down her wine glass. 'I'll see myself out.'

She closed his door gently but decisively behind her. The ante-room was empty.

She stood for a moment with her back to the door. Then she opened it quickly and marched in.

Eden had his back to her and was standing staring out of the window. When he heard her entrance, he turned round abruptly.

'Oh, it's you again.'

'Are you surprised?' Charmian walked to where he stood. Her face had a graver, harder look now. 'You didn't think I'd really gone, did you? Have a look at this photograph again, please. And now look at this one too.' She held out the picture of the dead figure of Josh Fox who was really Edward Elder. 'Do you know him? You do, don't you?'

A grey colour had crept into Leonard Eden's face.

'He's dead too, Mr Eden. He too was murdered.'

'I didn't know that.' He sank down into the chair behind him, knocking over the glass of wine which Charmian had not finished so that wine and water stained his trousers. He stared at the stain without touching it.

I was right about the soft centre, Charmian thought. A lot of deep emotion here, more than he can control. He's trained himself to be one sort of person, but he can't keep it up now.

'For some time,' said Charmian, 'I have had the feeling that there was someone unidentified in this case. Someone unnamed pulling the strings. I think that person was you.'

The breeze blew through the window, disturbing the curtains, but for a measurable moment neither of them spoke. Charmian was determined not to break the silence.

'I did know Vivien,' said Leonard Eden in a low voice. 'I knew her. And as you've guessed, I knew Josh Fox as well.'

Charmian picked the glass off the floor and put it on the windowsill. 'Come on, you can't leave it there.'

'I don't know how much you know, or have put together. I loved Vivien, but I have a wife. I love her too, respect her for what she is, but my feelings for Vivien were . . .' He seemed to have difficulty with his words. 'Quite uncontrollable,' he

164

said at last. 'Sounds trite, doesn't it? I expect you might say that I would have got over it. But I didn't and I hadn't.'

'It was you who arranged her move to Dulcet Road?'

'Yes. You could almost say that I bought up Bloods so that Vivien could have Dulcet Road. But it wasn't quite like that. Not so simple. Nothing ever is, of course.'

'No.' She thought that with him, business would always be business. It would not necessarily come first, it would be slipped into its appropriate place but it would never be totally overlooked. 'Were you going to leave your wife and marry Vivien?'

'I think so.'

'Or was it just Vivien who thought so?'

'No.' His voice was firmer. 'It was both of us.'

'But it was going to take time?'

'Yes.' He was surprised now. 'You know?'

'I've heard the story before.'

'Ah. Yes, I'm not pretending to be original. We weren't, Viv and I.' He spoke with some dignity. 'As a story it's old hat, isn't it?'

'I'm sorry. I shouldn't have spoken like that.'

'No, don't be. I like you for speaking out, for taking the woman's side. Thank you.'

Oddly enough, she believed him, and it silenced her in her turn.

Across the room the bank of screens, which had been almost quietly conversing with themselves, suddenly burst into agitated life.

Charmian saw them. 'The stockmarket's crashed. Or an atomic bomb has dropped.'

He barely turned his head. 'Just New York coming into the market.' Or San Francisco or Taiwan or another outpost whose voice had to be listened to.

'I didn't kill her. I loved her and the child.'

'Ah yes, the child.'

'I wanted Vivien and the child. I grieve for the loss of that child as much as for her.'

'You know how she died?'

165

'Yes. I was in the house.'

'Of course, you must have a set of keys. But the locks were changed.'

'I simply helped myself to keys from Bloods, when my own set did not work. They are not too careful with their keys.'

'I noticed. What did you think you were doing?'

'I knew she'd been killed. I had someone watching her.' Josh Fox.

'Why did you have her watched? She wasn't going to run away.' Or was she, poor Viv?

He took a deep breath. 'I thought she might be tempted to have an abortion. I didn't want that. I wanted to know. Fox had orders to stop her. Or anyway tell me.'

He had Charmian silenced once again. But she knew how to be cruel.

'Did you know that she probably wouldn't have had the child anyway? It came up in the post mortem. There was something wrong. The embryo was malformed.'

He closed his eyes and took a deep breath. Charmian let the silence last a moment, then she spoke:

'You say you went to the house when you knew she had been found dead? Yes?'

He nodded. 'Her body had gone, but the room hadn't been cleaned up. Not totally. There was no one around. There may have been a man on the front, but I got in round the back, the way I always used.'

'Was it your blood there?'

'Yes. I cut myself.'

'On what?'

'On one of the kitchen knives. It was an accident. At least, I suppose it was. But I have thought that really I wanted my blood to mix with Vivien's.'

'Why did you go to the house? Not just to see where Vivien had been killed, don't give me that.' There had been signs of a search, she remembered, and a hurried departure. 'We missed you there, Dolly and I,' she thought. 'The case could have ended at that point.'

166

He looked down at his hands. 'There were photographs, letters, private things. I knew where Vivien had hidden them.'

Self-preservation operating, she thought, but still not passing judgement on him. But Dolly would not be pleased to know what the first searchers had overlooked.

'But you still say you did not kill her?'

'I swear it.' He was sweating now. He got up and pushed the window open more widely. 'I'd been out of the country. Straight off a flight. You can check that.'

'We will, of course. Where were you?'

'Geneva,' he said. 'I can't remember the number of the flight, but my secretary will know.'

Things can be fudged, thought Charmian, given money and power.

'What do you think was the motive for Vivien's murder?'

He shook his head. 'I don't know.'

'But it must have been connected with your relationship with her.'

'I don't know that.'

'Seems likely to me.'

'What about those women? The ones she had made friends with? They sounded a very weird outfit to me.'

'Oh, you know about them?'

'Of course. Josh Fox told me.'

'He was working for you, yet you attacked him. You did, didn't you?'

'Yes.' He put a hand to his face. 'And now he's dead. I didn't kill him either.'

'Why did you beat him up?'

'I thought he lied to me. He didn't do his job properly or Vivien would not have been killed.'

Charmian considered this. She would leave it there for now. 'You'll have to make a statement.'

'Can I do it later? Tomorrow? I'm not going to run away. You can have my passport if you like.'

'That won't be necessary. I'll make an arrangement for you to come in. Probably to Alexandria Road in Windsor. You

167

know where that is? You'd better bring your lawyer with you.'

'You're making this sound very final somehow,' he muttered.

'Have you told your wife anything of this?' He shook his head. 'Then you'd better.' And soon, she thought. But not too soon. I might want to see her myself.

As she turned to go, he said, 'How did you get on to me?'

Charmian walked towards the door before she spoke. 'You were described to me,' she said. 'By a woman looking out of a window.'

And I shall want to know what you were doing there watching that house in Woodstock Close.

At Woodstock Close Miss Jessamon was discreetly examining Denise Flaxon's rooms. Her own key fitted the door, always had, a little something she never mentioned, but in any case she had promised Denise to keep an eye on her rooms because they both had this feeling that there was someone getting into this house who should not be there. That is, she had said so and Denise had agreed. No sign of disturbance in the room, all tidy, too neat really, so that she decided sadly that Denise would never stay. She didn't look like a stayer.

Selling face creams was no career for a woman like her. She needed a home, you could tell. Flo Jessamon had long years of emotional deprivation behind her and knew the signs.

Charmian had not finished her enquiries for the day. A quiet look in the telephone book and a check with the receptionist, who was by now too dazed by Charmian to resist, had produced Leonard Eden's home address. She could have got it from him directly, he would have given it, but she wanted to see his wife and what might be called his home ground before he had time to send out a warning. He wouldn't be doing anything of the kind for a little while yet, she calculated. If ever she had met a man in the process of sorting himself out, Leonard Eden, when last seen, had been that man.

A look at where he lived would be valuable. You could tell a lot about a man if you got a sight of his house before he knew you were coming.

The Eden home was on a quiet road not far from Ascot. Not Surrey after all then, but not so far away. There was no ostentation about it, but an air of solid worth and wealth. Its neighbours bore out this impression as far as could be observed because all sheltered behind high hedges or neat brick walls with closed gates. A closed gate which opened electronically always bespoke a good income.

But the gate to the Eden house was open. Leonard Eden might have preferred it that way, he seemed that sort.

Charmian drove in slowly, the short gravelled drive taking her up to the front of the white house. It was so white and immaculate that Charmian felt grubbier and more untidy than she actually was. She took the opportunity to comb her hair and add some lipstick.

Between the drive and the house there was a crescent-shaped bed where bush roses and standard roses alternated in red and white. A woman in a large sun hat was kneeling among the roses weeding.

She got up and came towards Charmian, removing her gardening gloves and putting them neatly into the pocket of the apron she wore. The apron was of a kind of sacking with *Laura's Garden* embroidered across the front, and it protected a green linen dress, conservative in cut but expensive-looking. The woman and the house matched.

'Good afternoon?' It was a pretty face, pale-skinned with big blue eyes and neat features discreetly made up, and framed in the sun hat with a little blonde hair escaping.

'Mrs Eden?'

'I am, do you want me?' She looked at the car, her face expressing doubt and caution. Charmian's car was at no time a thing of beauty and today looked dustier than ever.

Charmian got out of the car, experiencing an instant

and depressing reaction: she probably thinks I'm selling something. It told her what she must look like.

'Chief Superintendent Daniels. Can I talk to you?'

'What about?'

Charmian gave her the usual few words about it being just a routine enquiry and checking a few facts.

'But a Chief Superintendent?' she queried. 'And shouldn't there be two of you?'

'I'll go away if you like.' And come back with a pair. Your husband never questioned me.

'No. Come into the house.' She led the way. 'We'll use the sun room.'

Not quite in the house, kept just outside, Charmian was sat down in the pale blue chintz-covered chair in a glassed room with a Chinese rug on a flagged floor and blue and white plants in blue and white pots.

Her hostess sat down opposite her. 'I'm sorry, you took me by surprise. I'm Laura Eden.'

Ah, thought Charmian. The other L for EL? And possibly some of the money to start it in the beginning? Certainly a lot of the support. She looked, as far as Charmian could see her face beneath its sheltering hat, like a woman who would back her husband to the hilt.

'Tell me what you want, Miss Daniels. I think it must be important or you wouldn't be here.'

'We are often obliged to check people's movements in one of our enquiries. To eliminate them, really. It has to be done.' Charmian got out her notebook and pretended to study it. 'I believe your husband was away on the night of June Fourteenth? And came back the next day?'

'So it's Len you are asking about?' She sounded surprised. 'Let me think? Yes, he was in Switzerland, I think. But he's often away. Really for days and days at a time. It's part of his life. I'd need to look in my diary.'

'Would you do that, Mrs Eden?' Charmian sat back in her chair, not to be moved, waiting.

'Of course, excuse me while I get it.'

While Laura Eden was gone, Charmian prowled round

the sun room. Every plant was in beautiful order, not a slug-eaten leaf, not a fallen petal. This was a woman who knew about gardening. About everything domestic, probably.

An inner door led to a sitting room which was as beautifully arranged and as meticulously cared for as the garden and the sun room. It looked as though everything had its appointed place and stayed there. Not a house in which people romped or played games.

As she stood there, she dropped her notebook. It fell with a thud, scattering all the loose papers and letters which were always wedged inside. She was picking them up hastily as she heard Mrs Eden coming down the stairs.

Laura Eden held her diary in her hand. 'Yes, I can confirm that date.'

Charmian got up. 'Thank you, Mrs Eden. Sorry to have bothered you. But it had to be done.'

'I understand,' said Laura Eden doubtfully. 'I'd like to know what it's about, though.'

Charmian did not answer this question. Instead, she said, 'Have you spoken to your husband this afternoon, Mrs Eden?'

'No.'

'I think you should. He may need you.'

At that moment she thought she had seen all she wanted to of the Eden home. The house spoke very loudly of the life that Len Eden had lived there and it had been, from the evidence of his more generously disordered office, not the sort of life he totally wanted. She could begin to guess, perhaps, what Vivien had offered.

A childless house too, she thought as she drove away. She could see Laura Eden standing watching her.

'Why do I find you depressing, dear?' Charmian asked herself. 'And why do I call you "dear"? What is there about you?'

The figure behind her did not wave, just stood looking.

*

171

Charmian was ready to go back to Maid of Honour Row now and think things over in peace. Also a wash and a change of clothes seemed indicated. Not to mention food. And now she thought about it, there would be Muff also with her hungry face on. Had she let the cat out into the garden before she left in her hurry to see Dolly in Alexandria Road? She thought not. Another cause to speed home.

For once there were no hold-ups on the motorway and the traffic, although dense, was moving. She was back outside her house in record time. As she went in through her gate she observed that a pile of yellow sheets had been dumped by her gate. And guess by whom? she thought.

In the hall, she paused. 'Oh Muff, Muff, how could you?'

The cat had filled in the time of her imprisonment by shredding a newspaper, the pages of a book which she had knocked off a table (also upsetting a vase of lupins), and the letters which had come by the second post. The small remains of something banana-coloured lay in one corner, having received special teeth and claw attention.

There was no sign of Muff herself.

'Where are you, you beast?' Charmian advanced angrily towards the kitchen.

Kate appeared at the door. 'I just got back and found all this mess.' The cat had been at work in the kitchen too, but here she had contented herself with knocking objects off shelves. Nothing was broken, but several bottles and jars had spilled their contents so that herbs and juices were mixed on the floor. There was a strong smell of garlic. 'I've turned her out. I think she was glad to go.'

'I'll probably kill her,' said Charmian.

Kate was already clearing up the kitchen floor. Charmian looked down at her bent head. And where were you these last few days? she questioned silently. But I suppose I mustn't ask.

Kate gave an answer to what had not been asked. 'Been working in London at the V and A. Sorry I didn't let you know.'

You never do, said Charmian to herself.

172

'But I got so excited by William Morris. He really was great. I don't think I gave him full credit before.' Kate raised her head and looked solemnly at Charmian. 'I believe he will be a huge influence on me. I'm off to Kelmscott tomorrow.'

The nineteenth century had at last arrived in Kate's life. It had taken her some while to admit its artistic existence but now she had.

'I'm going to shower and change,' said Charmian.

'There's a message for you from Dolly. She's coming round.'

'Can you put a meal together?' Charmian was going up the stairs. 'Look in the freezer. Salad in the refrigerator. I think there's some cold chicken as well.' There should be, unless Muff had mysteriously got at it.

'How are the witches?' called Kate.

'Those ladies are quiet,' Charmian called back. And with plenty to occupy their thoughts and calm them down. Was the figure of Josh Fox haunting them? It ought to, because it haunted her.

While she was in the shower, the telephone rang and she heard Kate answer it.

Presently she called up the stairs: 'Dolly is not only coming round, she is bringing someone with her.'

She heard Dolly arriving while she was still dressing. There was a man with her, she could hear his voice and Kate's laughter. That was a good sign, anyone Kate laughed with could probably be trusted.

She threw her dirty clothes into the laundry bin, placed her notebook and papers on the bedside table and went downstairs.

Kate had tidied all the mess away by the simple expedient of sweeping it away into one corner, but the table was laid for a meal and she was mixing a salad.

'Chicken salad,' she said looking up. 'All I could do in ten minutes. And here is Dolly and this is George Rewley.'

She had that special note in her voice which said to her godmother: This man is of interest to me.

173

Dolly was leaning up against the sink, watching the man who was struggling to open a bottle of wine. She held up a friendly hand, but did not speak.

Not a tall young man – Kate in her heels was as tall if not taller. Square of shoulder and probably more muscular than he looked, but it was his face and even more his eyes that attracted attention.

He had a thin, bony face with clear grey eyes that studied you intently. Looking at you, Charmian felt, right through and out to the other side. She wasn't used to being transparent.

'This is a sparkling wine,' he said as he pulled at the cork. 'Going to go over everything when we do get it open.'

'Take it in the garden, you two,' ordered Charmian. Then she looked at Dolly with raised eyebrows. 'Well, what's all this?'

'Nice, isn't he?' Dolly selected a stick of celery to chew upon. 'I'm starving. Rewley is the only hearing member of his family of five, so that he is really into lip reading. Grew up doing it. He says it gives him an insight not only into what people are saying but also what they are not saying. The thought behind.' She chewed on the celery. 'Life's a perpetual whispering gallery to him, he picks up everything.'

'Terrifying,' said Charmian. 'He ought to have a good time with Kate.' Plenty not said there.

'So I sent him down to see Vivien Charles's parents, well, father and step, in Cuckfield. I thought he might pick up something we'd missed.'

'And did he?'

'He said that the house just oozed religion, crucifixes and bleeding hearts on the walls everywhere, and that behind all the outward grief the father and the stepmother claimed to feel – said they felt – he could see them saying "Vivien was a wicked girl and we're glad she died away from home." No love. He said he could understand how she'd fallen in with the witches, he'd have done the same himself.'

'Her grandmother was a witch so she claimed.' But

it helped explain her relationship with Len Eden too, Charmian thought. If you ever needed an explanation for sexual attraction. 'Then Rewley'd better watch out. They must be looking for a replacement for Josh Fox.'

'Anything else?' she asked. 'Are we any further forward?'

'I think we are. I've always wanted to understand Vivien better.'

'And I want to understand the killer,' said Charmian, watching the pair in the garden, that dedicated non-communicator, Kate, and Rewley, that constant reader of the subtext.

'There is one other thing,' said Dolly slowly. 'The father admitted to Rewley that he had lied, or rather suppressed a bit of the truth in his earlier interview. Vivien *had* been in touch with him in the weeks before her death. He told Rewley that Vivien had wanted to come back home. She said she was frightened; she acted as if she'd had a shock. They didn't let her come. That part was not said aloud, but he read it for himself. He could read their guilt.'

'What was she frightened of?'

'She said she was being watched.'

'So she was, of course,' said Charmian. And not only by Josh Fox which she might not have noticed, he was a professional after all. But the murderer had somehow declared his attentions and in a shocking way. The foetus had felt the force of that pain. 'I'll tell you about that. In fact, I've got plenty to tell you, too.'

She ran upstairs to get her notes. As she held the notebook something fell out of it.

She picked it up. A small dark-coloured hairgrip and caught in it a strand of coarse brown hair.

It must have been on the floor of the Eden's house so that she had picked it up when she retrieved her fallen papers.

She ran the hair through her fingers as she considered it. The hair felt stiff and dry. It said something to her.

Chapter Fifteen

'Stay behind,' Charmian said to Dolly when Kate decided that Rewley should be shown one of her favourite buildings in Windsor by moonlight. A new favourite, one she had not previously considered of much interest, but which now came to the top with her new enthusiasms for things Victorian. It was not a church or chapel or splendid house, but a railway station, and although Rewley pointed out that he knew, and indeed used it very often, Kate told him that he needed its delights pointed out by a trained eye. 'It represents a high point of Victorian building and engineering,' she said, 'before they got too heavy and Imperial. This is just a cosy little bit of domestic building, but done for a Queen and her husband.'

Rewley did not seem disinclined for the moonlight stroll, although he had not previously taken much interest in Queen Victoria's railway station. Charmian wondered what he could see behind Kate's spoken words apart from what was obvious to them all: that she liked him.

'Nice girl,' he said to Charmian as Kate disappeared to get a coat. 'But something's tearing her apart.'

'Oh, you've noticed?'

'She's shouting it out,' he said simply.

They had all eaten a happy dinner of chicken and salad in Charmian's kitchen, washed down with draughts of sparkling white wine. Muff had crept in from the garden and quietly taken part in the meal.

'I forgive you,' said Charmian, patting her head. 'Although many wouldn't.'

'She's forgiving you,' Kate said. 'It's that way round. Your fault.'

Over the meal George Rewley had told them all about his visit to Cuckfield. 'Nice little bungalow they've got, but what a pair. Anything crazy that happened to Vivien was partly their fault. Take my word for it. She must have had a terrible childhood, mental bullies is how I'd describe them and not much real love around. She was programmed to fall into trouble.'

'She had other help,' said Charmian sourly.

Dolly gave a little nod of agreement. 'Don't be a male you-know-what.'

'I'm not.'

Kate gave everyone a wide, radiant smile. Leave him to me, it said. He will be taught.

Charmian hoped for his own preservation that Rewley could read it too. It was the sort of smile that should carry a health warning. Watch my lips, I could be dangerous.

'I wanted them to go,' Dolly said as the two departed. 'I told Rewley to fix it.'

Charmian laughed. 'And he did, he's what you said and a cunning beggar as well.' Kate might have met her match.

'Oh, Rewley's all of that. He can be hard to work with, but I find him useful. He'll mellow with age.' He was about three years younger than Dolly, but had come straight into the police from school. Charmian thought that she didn't see him mellowing exactly, but he might learn to mask his cleverness.

'Now let's talk things over,' said Dolly. 'Tomorrow I have a conference with Elman and Father. I don't think Father will give any trouble, he's still playing politics, but Fred Elman could be awkward. He's all at sixes and sevens since Josh Fox was killed,' she went on gloomily. 'And of course, he's got that damned Peter Arbat on his back. Well, we all have, Pete can be a swine, but I can see his point. The two cases are one case and one murderer must have done both killings. I've got to have something reasoned out to tell them.'

'You've read my notes?'

'I need to sort out what it means.' Dolly shook her head. 'I can't see the answer. I still fancy it being one of the women, Caprice possibly, she's beginning to look a very doubtful character. Not a record exactly but she's sailed close to the wind in knowing drug pushers once or twice. But there's no case, really, I see that . . . I'd settle for it being the man Eden myself. I think we could get evidence there.'

Charmian said, 'Don't look for easy answers, there's been too much lying.'

'Arbat's raising trouble, he's got it in for the witches and he may be right.'

'What's Arbat's history?'

'He transferred here from the North. Newcastle, I think, but that was before my time. Not a Geordie, though, not from the way he speaks. Supposed to have said he wanted to work in the south of England, wanted to specialise in drugs. Rumour has it someone wanted to shoot him, and that was the real reason.'

'Because he was too clever for them?'

Dolly laughed. 'No, because he was having it off with the wrong person's wife. He got out in time. He was clever enough for that.'

'Is he married?'

'Of course, he is,' said Dolly. 'Sometimes she lives with him and sometimes she doesn't. You can't blame her. I think it's off at the moment.'

'Is it drugs he has against the witches?'

'Yes, Caprice and Twickers, in particular.'

'Could be,' said Charmian. She was almost sure that the little manikins dropped on her doorstep came from Caprice. Malice? Or to frighten her off? Bad psychology, if so. That was why she thought it must be Caprice, she was a stupid woman at base, whereas Birdie and Winifred were, in their own way, sharp judges of the world.

'I think so myself. Oh well, we'll get to know, I suppose, if we look hard enough . . . Arbat thinks that's why her place was broken into. Someone looking for drugs.'

'I don't think so,' said Charmian.

178

'That reminds me,' said Dolly. 'About Josh Fox's records . . . Hard to know what to call him, isn't it? I hate these double identity tricks. Yes, he did keep records, in his own way, of course. I don't think they would have won him any prizes in a literature class but they served his purpose. Brief and concise. And there were a few photographs. He kept everything in one old filing cabinet and that had been searched, and several files removed. Must be what his killer came for.' Dolly's voice was quiet. It was amazing, and sad, how the figure of Josh Fox diminished as he was investigated. Not so much to admire there, after all. Just a bonny face and perhaps a seedy spirit behind it. She didn't like admitting it to herself, but it looked like it.

Charmian cut across her thoughts. 'Fingerprints?'

'Nothing useful at the moment, but it's early days.'

Charmian considered: Forensics give you a lead, could get you into court with a proveable case, but it was the face-to-face contact with all those in the case that counted in the long run.

She poured some coffee for them both while Dolly studied her notes again.

'Where are you having your conference with Fred Elman and Father?'

'In Father's room, I believe. He hates to stir unless he has to.'

'While this is happening, I want to set up an interview with Leonard Eden in Alexandria Road. I want someone with me. Who can I have?'

Dolly considered. 'You might as well have Rewley.'

'He could have quite a future, that young man.'

'Yes,' said Dolly, who hoped she had a distinguished professional career ahead of her herself, but who felt she was having a downturn at the moment. 'You can't tell though, can you? People burn out . . .'

They looked at each other. 'Women more than men?' Dolly was asking. 'Come on, you're the expert on women and their sufferings.'

'Surely not,' Charmian said. 'Not us.'

'I feel it sometimes.'

'But that's just when you mustn't say it aloud.'

Next day, the hall in Alexandria Road seemed quiet as Charmian waited for Leonard Eden to arrive. She was prepared for him.

An early call from Dolly Barstow had confirmed what she already knew.

'Eden did not come back on that flight from Geneva as he said he did. He had the booking and it was not cancelled, but he was not on the plane. We believe he caught a late-night flight. He had another booking as a stand-by passenger. No evidence where he went from Heathrow, but he was around and could have done the killing. So he lied,' Dolly said.

'I knew he'd lied,' said Charmian. 'Think about the scene in which Vivien was found, the set-up around, the vomit in the sink, and you will see why I knew.'

George Rewley was there before her in Alexandria Road, standing, arms folded, studying the room. Listening in to conversations, she had to believe. No wonder his colleagues were nervous with him.

'Every time I'm with you I feel as though I know what reading between the lines means.'

'You mustn't believe all you hear,' he said with a serious face.

She laughed, it was a good riposte. He was a comic as well as an observer. 'You're not telling me you don't lip read?'

'The stories don't lose in the telling . . . but yes, I do it without thinking. Habit. But for the rest, well, it's a question of looking closely at the face, watching the muscles move. Everyone does it to some extent, you do yourself. I just do it more. I've had the practice.'

'Keep it up,' said Charmian, 'and tell me what you see. But leave my face out of it.'

'This Leonard Eden who's coming in, he's prime suspect for the murder?'

'You could say so.' Leonard Eden had certainly lied to her, and lied again.

Rewley let his eyes dwell on her face and drew his own conclusions. 'But you're not saying so.'

Charmian did not answer. She was beginning to feel that Rewley inhibited speech. She compromised. Head down, looking at her notes.

'He's coming in with his solicitor.'

From his place by the window with its view into the junction of Alexandria Road and King Street, Rewley said: 'Tallish, balding chap, is he?'

'Sounds like him.' She looked at the clock. On time. As she would have expected with Leonard Eden.

'I have news for you: no solicitor. He's on his own.'

'Damn.'

'Does it matter?'

'It would have been better. I'm going to ask sensitive questions. Don't want to be accused of bullying a witness. Never mind, he's here now.'

Leonard Eden, who looked as though he had not slept and might never sleep again, came straight up to her. 'I want to say this now before we start: I gather you've seen my wife. You spoke to her last night?'

'That's right.'

'I don't want her . . .' he hesitated, 'more disturbed than she has been already.'

'It's a bit late for that, Mr Eden.'

He remained silent. Possibly Rewley could read something in his face, she herself could not.

'Why didn't you bring a solicitor with you? I advised you to.'

'I didn't want him here. Later will do.'

'I think you need all the help you can get.'

In a low voice he said, 'I accept responsibility for everything.'

'You lied to me yesterday.'

'I admit it. I killed Vivien.'

'That isn't the lie I meant.'

181

He looked at her warily, caught off his guard.

'There was another lie. You went not once but twice to Dulcet Road, the first time you found her lying there dead. That was when you cut your hand, when you moved various objects placed around her, and then vomited in the sink.'

Len Eden moved his gaze towards the window.

'You always leave a *carte de visite* of your presence, Mr Eden. You left one in the shop, Twickers.'

'Twickers?'

'If it was your blood in Dulcet Road, it was also you in Twickers,' said Charmian bluntly. 'What were you doing there? Those women had nothing to do with killing Vivien.'

'Around her body . . .' he murmured. 'Those horrible objects, it spoke of them. I wanted to find out.'

Charmian shook her head. 'No, think about the other lie you told me and face the truth.'

'What lie?'

No doubt about the wariness now. Was he regretting the lack of a lawyer? He seemed to be bracing himself for what was to come.

Charmian forced herself on, it was like cutting into bleeding flesh. 'The other lie was about why you hired Josh Fox. It was not to prevent Vivien having an abortion, that wasn't going to happen, but to find out if she herself was being followed. You wanted to protect her. And I know from whom.'

She stood up. 'DC Rewley will take your statement. I think you'd better call your lawyer. You may be here some time.'

Rewley followed her to the door. 'Supposing he asks to call his wife?'

'Tell him he can't.'

'Right.'

'And keep him here.'

'You don't think he'd kill his wife, do you?'

'I think she may be dead already.'

A sub-conversation was going on between them. You've dropped me in it, he was saying. This is something more than I've ever handled.

Do you good, Charmian was saying back.

'He's dead himself to my eyes,' Rewley said. 'Dead from the inside out.'

'I'm afraid so.'

Charmian drove at once to the Eden house near Ascot. She knew she must speak to Laura Eden. The woman was in a most dangerous position. The question was, Charmian thought, whether she cared. She knew all right, but perhaps no longer minded.

Yes, she must care, the need to survive was demonstrably strong. She had lied for her husband, had fought for him, she would certainly fight for herself.

What shall I say to her? Shall I begin by saying: Do you know a woman with curly dark hair called Denise Flaxon?

The house, when she got there, was silent. No one answered her bell. She walked round the house, looking into the ground-floor windows. Nothing to be seen.

She left the house behind her and searched the garden, noticing once again the beautiful order in which it was kept. Even today the lawns were close-cropped and immaculately tidy with not a leaf spoiling their sheen.

She went back to the house for one last look round. Nothing had changed. She could see through to the kitchen which was empty. If anyone had eaten breakfast there today then they had been tidy eaters and had cleared away neatly. She tried to look through the letterbox but her vision was blocked by a pile of letters.

Was Laura Eden in there, but keeping silent?

Or dead? Dead already.

Charmian sat in her car debating what to do. She had noticed a telephone box down the road; she went to it and made a call.

★

In Woodstock Close, Flo Jessamon was saying goodbye to Denise Flaxon. She had an idea that Denise would have slipped away without a word, but naturally Flo wasn't having any of that.

If you didn't say goodbye a relationship was never really closed as it should be. Moreover, in the case of the flat on the top floor, it left her with the uneasy feeling that the flat was never truly empty. Not quite inhabited but not quite clear, either. As it happened, it was that sort of flat.

So she waited for Denise on the stairs. Caught her, you could say. She could see on Denise's face the feeling that she had been captured.

'You off, dear?'

'Yes. I'm moving away.'

Flo waited hopefully to be told where but no such information was forthcoming. I'd have said if it was me, she told herself. It's good manners. But people can be very hurtful.

'What about the post?' she asked.

'I've arranged that,' said Denise. 'I'll leave my keys with you.'

'Oh, there was a message for you, dear. I nearly forgot to mention it.' Not true at all, she had been saving it up. 'That policewoman. I don't believe you met her, the nice one called Daniels, she wants to see you. I suppose it's about that body you found, you poor thing. Yes, I know about that, we all do but didn't like to say. There's still got to be an inquest, hasn't there? You'll be a witness. Do let me know if I can help.' Let her see you've got good manners, even if she hasn't, Flo told herself. 'Miss Daniels asked if you were here, I told her you weren't. You weren't just then, dear. I have the address and the telephone number.' She had remembered them for herself too as a matter of interest. Alexandria Road and a Windsor number. 'Or she'd come here.'

'I won't make her do that,' said Denise, wishing that there had been nobody in her life. People did make trouble, alive or dead. She was a witness to a death, always had been and always would be. She should have missed that encounter. Why hadn't she? Somehow life had pushed her into it.

It was a horrible thing, being a witness to a death.

'Look after yourself, dear,' said Flo Jessamon. 'I've always felt nervous for you.' The woman who saw too much, she said to herself, with a delicious shiver.

I could die and no one would miss me, thought Denise as she drove away towards Slough. But I believe that woman would. A faint feeling of friendliness stirred inside. Very faint and it soon faded away. I wish I could have done more for her skin, she thought. Too late now.

Denise drove herself to a small motel on the outskirts of Windsor where she booked a room. She had not been there before but she could see it was the sort of quiet, boring place where no one took much interest in you. She wanted to be part of a company where the company she kept did not notice she was there.

She made herself some tea from the equipment in one corner of the room. In truth the room seemed all corners, but it may just have been the way she was feeling.

Cornered.

She admired herself for being able to make that joke.

After the tea, she found her mind had cleared: she must see this detective. Some situations will not go away and clearly this was one.

She washed her face and hands, attended to her hair and make-up, debated how she should look, made a decision, then set out.

More time had passed than she had taken in, it was getting dusky, but she would find Charmian Daniels in Alexandria Road or somewhere and get it all over.

She felt brave, but exceedingly cold. Odd considering how hot the day had been. Somewhere in this journey of hers, her bones had been taken out and something else put in their place. The cold bit.

Tomorrow, she told herself, I shall be a new person and drive away for ever.

Charmian went back to Alexandria Road where she talked to Dolly. Rewley had gone. She learnt that Leonard Eden was being held at the best protected police station in Prince Consort Road. There were plenty of press around and several TV teams, Dolly reported soberly, hence the need for protection.

'How were Elman and Father?'

'Manageable. Both got other things on their minds. Unspecified, but I could tell. They hate the thought of dealing with Leonard Eden, he seems to have wires leading to all high-powered centres.'

'I don't think he'll try and use them.'

'No,' said Dolly. 'I feel that too. Except you can't tell. He's not making a fuss, but he's holding his own . . . And he did try to get in touch with his wife, but no answer.'

'As I discovered.'

'He didn't seem too surprised. I wondered if he was putting on an act.'

'Could be,' said Charmian.

Dolly got up and took a little walk around her desk. Charmian could sometimes irritate her when she was too enigmatic.

'We'll have to let him go soon. Can't hold him with what we've got. You don't think he's killed her already?'

'She might be dead,' said Charmian. 'Don't keep walking round the desk. It annoys me. No sign of Mrs Flaxon?'

Dolly shook her head.

'I'll come back. Hang on to her if she turns up.'

'Will do.'

She did indeed come back towards the end of the afternoon. Dolly detached herself from a group and shook her head.

'Not here?' said Charmian. She wasn't surprised. 'I'm worried about her.'

The two of them left together. Dolly was going to the opera, Charmian going home.

'I hope I don't get called away. The tickets cost about a hundred pounds,' said Dolly. 'Besides I want to see the new Carmen.'

At the end of the road they prepared to part, Dolly to drive one way and Charmian another. Most of the other cars parked there all day had gone, but one remained.

'Where are Kate and Rewley?' Charmian asked as they left each other.

'I think they're still reading each other's lips,' said Dolly absently.

'That could last quite a time with Kate. But not for ever. I hope Rewley knows that.'

The house in Maid of Honour Row was quiet and empty. No Kate. So probably Dolly was right and she was with George Rewley.

But no Muff either, and that was a pity. Too much freedom for Muff went to her head and made her ungovernable. She was bad enough, anyway. All cats were roaring egotists, it was only to be expected, but Muff beat all.

She went to the back door and called. No Muff.

She opened the front door and could see the front garden was empty of cats, but the creature sometimes crossed the road to forbidden territory.

It was a nice evening, calm and still, the sort that Wordsworth liked. Down the road she could see Birdie Peacock and Winifred Eagle accompanied by several young girls. They were apprentice witches, Birdie was starting her Junior League. The police had sent them home with the caution that this was not the end of it, but not to worry too much. All in all Birdie thought it was the time for new beginnings.

But not all her recruits had a very clear idea what they were joining and their motives were mixed. One girl thought it was a kind of Brownie pack and she knew Miss Peacock made very good cakes. Another girl had been forcibly joined by her mother who wanted to get her out of the house and anything would do, while yet another girl was present because she wanted to leave home and never see her mother again. The fourth girl knew what it was all about and had come because she desired to learn a spell that would get her through her GCSEs, or, alternatively, put her father into a deep sleep for several years so he would never notice she had failed, either would do.

Charmian saw them distantly down the road, the castle silhouetted behind them, as she went to the gate to look for Muff. The cat slid out of the shadow of the hedge and up the garden path.

As Charmian followed the cat up to the house, another person came up behind her. She turned quickly.

'Miss Daniels?'

A woman with a froth of dark curls, eyes more grey than blue as seen in the dusk, bright lipstick and softly pink cheeks. She was wearing a frilly cotton blouse over a printed skirt. Her white shoes were set on high slender heels which made her as tall as Charmian.

'I'm Mrs Flaxon.'

'Ah,' Charmian drew in a breath. 'I thought you might be. How did you know where to find me?' She did not broadcast her address.

'I'd just got to Alexandria Road when I saw you driving off. I followed. I've been sitting in the car waiting.'

Charmian nodded towards the open door. Muff was sitting on the threshold looking out. 'Come in.'

'Wait a minute, let me just get my breath back.' Denise sounded as if she was hyperventilating.

That'll make two of us, thought Charmian, feeling her heart beating fast.

From her seat at the door, Muff had caught sight of Benedict, black cat, neighbour and enemy, entering the garden gate. The fur rose round her neck and her tail thickened.

'I wish I knew where I was going,' said Denise Flaxon, not taking up the offer to go into the house.

'Why not go home? If you've got one. Have you got one, Mrs Flaxon? Or is it Ms Flaxon? Or something else altogether?'

'You're laughing at me.' Denise's right arm moved and Charmian saw the flash of the knife.

She jumped back, at the same time trying to reach the

188

stabbing arm. As the two women jostled the black wig had slipped a fraction to reveal the blonde hair beneath. In that moment of urgent danger, Charmian saw it happen.

Before her eyes, they had all fused together, all three women, becoming one.

The dark-haired woman who had been created as a persona, who had cried in a room in Woodstock Close because there was someone lost inside that face who wanted to get out. A dark-haired beauty who had been so ambivalent that Flo Jessamon had felt the presence in that house of someone unacknowledged.

The fair-haired woman who had put on the dark wig, but who had changed out of it and into her own clothes in a public lavatory in Slough so she could go home as herself, who had created this other self to kill. To kill for revenge and jealousy and hate of the girl who had stolen her husband, who had stolen her life. This double person who had put witchcraft symbols around her victim partly to incriminate the witches, but also out of hate.

And the red-haired woman in jeans who had knifed Josh Fox, who had been hired to find out if she was threatening Vivien Charles, and who had a file on this woman which he was prepared to use for blackmail. He had watched her in Woodstock Close and her husband had watched him, watching her. Her husband, who had then attacked Fox because he had not been totally truthful about finding Denise Flaxon, who was also Laura Eden.

Muff saw Benedict strolling up the garden path and in a rush of fury hurled herself forward, screaming loudly. She looked twice her normal size and was three times as strident. Ben screamed back. Battle was joined.

The sudden noise made Charmian lose her balance and the knife went into the right arm, piercing an artery. The blood began to pump out.

Like a film, a rapid succession of events began to run before her. Love, hate, blackmail. With Leonard Eden trying to find out if his wife was watching Vivien, identifying who Denise Flaxon was, but still loving his wife too much

189

to accuse her of murder. Protecting both women, and failing both of them.

Charmian staggered backwards, holding her arm. She knew she had to stop the blood, but she was beginning to feel cold and dizzy.

This was it, then, this was how you went. In your own front garden in the middle of a cat fight.

Down the road, just about to turn the corner from Maid of Honour Row into the street where Miss Eagle lived, the band of apprentice witches and their leaders heard the noise.

'That's my Ben's voice,' said Winifred Eagle. She ran towards the sound of the fight. The rest followed, surging through the gate just as a tall woman with dishevelled hair tried to leave.

Charmian was slumped, half sitting, half lying, against the hedge. The fighting cats bounced away, leaping and screaming, carefully not damaging each other as they fell into the rosebed.

'Stop her,' gasped Charmian. The garden was growing dark but she could hear acutely.

A couple of the apprentices held on to the woman. To their surprise, her dark curls fell on to their hands. As she struggled, one contact lens fell out, so that the woman seemed to have one eye that was blueish, one that was brown and a kind of dark round tear on her cheek. She was a macabre spectacle. It was frightening, but they hung on. This was better than anything they had hoped for.

Birdie knelt by Charmian's side. She placed firm, cool fingers on the wound in Charmian's arm. 'I'll stop the bleeding, dear,' she said in a soothing voice. Out of the darkness now falling upon her, Charmian heard her say, 'I have the power to heal.'

In the distance, Winifred was calling her cat. 'If I could laugh,' thought Charmian, deep inside herself, 'I would.'

*

'You did,' said Dolly. 'I don't know if you know, but you were carried into hospital roaring with laughter.'

It was a day later, and early evening. Charmian had returned home from the hospital that afternoon.

The two women were in the sitting room of the house in Maid of Honour Row. Out in the kitchen Kate and Rewley were preparing supper. The evening sunlight came through the open window, where Muff sat washing her face with a contented look. Her dishful had been tasty tonight, and although the pair doing the cooking did not yet know it, they were missing a prawn or two.

Charmian leaned back against the cushion, feeling spoilt and cared for.

'It was my bad arm, you know. The one that has caused me all this trouble. And now, would you believe it, apart from being sore it's working perfectly.' She held up her right hand. 'This hand will write. I could write a book. Probably I won't but I could. Cured by a witch. Must be something in this witchcraft, Merrywick-style.'

'Birdie Peacock's very pleased with herself, I must try her on my eczema, although it feels better,' said Dolly.

She touched her face, yes, smooth and cool. She was pleased with life. It looked as though this case, code-named FANTASY, had been good for her. The big chief himself, the Chief Constable, had congratulated her.

'We've nailed Caprice, by the way. Arbat got a search warrant and a couple from the Drug Squad popped in. They caught her trying to flush her hoard down the drains. She'd had LSD and grass underneath the floor boards. She was as tight as an owl apparently. Whisky.'

'So Arbat's satisfied? And Fred Elman?'

'Delighted. Got his name in print. Still handling the Edens with extreme care, though. Not clear what's going to happen to Eden himself. He could be charged with the Twickers break-in, but he probably won't be.' Dolly shook her head. 'Laura Eden's in a very odd state. She'll get away with unfit to plead, I think.'

'It's always dangerous to be two persons,' said Charmian.

191

'It loosens up all sorts of interior forces. You never know who's going to come on top, Jekyll or Hyde.'

The interplay between husband and wife was strange and strong, a story in itself: he would save her if he could. He had known she might kill Vivien and had hired Josh Fox to watch his wife and protect the girl, yet when she did kill Vivien, and he knew she had, he still did not want her condemned.

Kate put her head round the door. 'The meal won't be long, but I'm just sending Rewley out for a few more prawns. I thought we had more than we have.'

She disappeared, then came back with a letter. 'Oh, this was just delivered by hand.'

Charmian took it. The envelope was of thick and beautiful paper, a pale rich cream, a pleasure to touch. The address was beautifully typed with the kind of archaic print one hardly ever saw now, almost like engraving.

She turned it over, she knew the crest on the back. You saw it every time the Royal Standard fluttered above the castle.

She hesitated to open it, wondering what it contained.

An invitation to a party? She opened it and read. No, not a party. Or not that sort.

'My goodness,' she thought. 'Who'd have believed it. Yes, I could help there, a crime like that would be a real tease. And with dogs too!'

Crime at the castle?

Canine crime?